Gem Hunter

An Alex Kustodia Mystery

by

Vicki Vass

For information, email Tedeschi Publishing, vicki@vickivass.com, or visit our website at: vickivass.com.

ISBN: 978-0-9989893-1-0

Printed in the United States of America

1 2 3 4 5 6 7 8 9 10

DEDICATION

To Amy Pedicini, an incredible jewelry designer and artist, who shares my love of gemstones and inspired me to write about colored stones. I marvel at my ring every time I look at it.

A special thanks to Victoria Finlay for writing *Jewels: A Secret History* and Aja Raden for writing *Stoned: Jewelry, Obsession, and How Desire Shapes the World*

Chapter One

Darkness. My pupils fully dilate, searching for any last remnant of light. I find none. My lungs expand, gasping for oxygen. Each time they do, I feel a sharp pain; my ribs are broken. I have lost feeling in my arms, my legs, my feet. My internal gyroscope is spinning, trying to find a direction. I find none. As I cough up the dust, my lungs catch fire. How long have I been like this?

I know I'm inverted because I can feel the weight of my body pushing against my lungs. How long has it been? How long until my body kills me? Twenty hours. Twenty-two hours. How long does it take until my blood pools into my lungs, suffocating me? My body is trying to kill me. The ancient Romans crucified their victims upside down to inflict this kind of long, painful death.

Blood is pooling in my brain. I'm starting to lose consciousness. I calm the raging terror that is rising within me. The fear will take me before the mine does. I slow my breathing. My heart still pumps hard, struggling to send blood to my legs. I can now feel the searing pain in my left shoulder. It's dislocated. I still have movement in my fingers, which are above me pressed against my hips. I wiggle my fingers in a circle. I sense there's an opening just above me. Out of my reach. My legs are either broken or trapped.

Thousands of tons of pegmatite crusted with precious gems like cloves on an Easter ham now bury me alive. I have told no one where I am. No help will come. I'm here illegally. The government closed these mines years ago in Vishnakahaputnam, India, yet still tribal miners continue to sneak in. Last year, forty miners were killed by a similar cave-in. I'd come to these mines to hunt the elusive alexandrite, one of the world's most rare stones. My father had warned me not to come here. A fool's mission, he'd called it. He should know. He had mined alexandrite in the neighboring Ural Mountains of Russia in the 1960s. The region where the stone was originally discovered in the 1880s. Those mines have long been depleted, but the same vein as in the Ural Mountains in the north runs into India, and that's what brought me here. For me, the reward is worth the risk.

Drops of saltwater drip over my legs, across my chest, and into my mouth. I close my lips as tightly as I can. I can feel the flow of air from above. Five hours. It's been five hours since the mine collapsed. That's what my internal clock is telling me. I think about my father and my grandfather, the only people who will miss me. I think about my bones buried here for decades, maybe centuries. Eventually I'll become part of the rock that I was seeking.

Seven hours. It's been seven hours. I lost consciousness for a short time. My breathing is shallow. The pain intensifies. The pain keeps me alive, keeps me alert. The water is loosening the rocks around me. I can move my left arm. My shoulder is twisted under my chin. If I can dislocate it further, I might get better leverage to push the rocks. With the strength I have left, I push my shoulder farther under my chin. I can feel and hear the bone snap. It doesn't matter anymore. I'm past pain. With my free arm, I push the rocks away from the opening three feet above me.

I twist my hips back and forth. More rocks tumble

past me. I'm free. I land flat on the floor of the mine, waiting for the blood to return to my legs and to my arms. I can feel my legs, and I can move them. My legs aren't broken. I crawl away from the pit that entrapped me. I follow the stream of saltwater that will lead me out of the mine. Eight hours without light, and my eyes can't adjust. I know I'm holding my hand inches in front of my face, but I can't see it. I can't even make out the shadow of the outline. I can feel my breath on the skin. I'm in complete blindness. I take a moment to clear my mind. I don't fear death. I don't fear the darkness. I accept the choices I make to live my life the way I do. What I fear is the pain I leave for the people I leave behind.

I crawl along the floor of the mine, pushing away the small rocks. There's not enough room for me to stand. Reaching over my head, I can feel the ceiling of the small crevice. I should never have journeyed this far back into the mine.

I pull myself along with my good arm, the jagged rocks cutting my skin. I don't know what I'll find at the end of this tunnel. If the mine entrance has collapsed, there's no other way out. I crawl for hours, my clothes shredding against the rocks. Saltwater stings the cuts on my arms and face. It's been twenty hours since the mine collapsed. The entrance can't be more than a hundred yards away. I still don't see any light. The fear rises in me again. I remember my father telling me about when he was trapped with his brother in the Ural Mountains. Seven days in darkness. No food or water. My father's leg was shattered. He still carried his brother through the rubble, searching for that elusive glimpse of light. He lasted seven days with a shattered leg. I can do this. I continued crawling.

Fifty yards. It can't be more than fifty yards, half

the length of a football field. The passageway is getting smaller. I have to squeeze through, first one arm in front, pulling me along, inches at a time. I think about the time. It must be morning in Chicago. My father will be at his small kitchen above the store, sipping his black tea through a sugar cube in his mouth, raspberry jam on his black beard. How long has it been since I've eaten? It's a good sign that I'm hungry. It's been days since I've eaten.

I pause, sitting back on my heels, hitting my head against the rocks above. I sink back down. I must continue. Twenty-five yards. At least twenty-five yards. The tunnel ends blocked by a pile of rocks. The opening is collapsed. Is it twenty-five yards? Is it twenty yards? How far do I have to dig? Can I even dig my way out? I start moving the rocks, one at a time, pushing them behind me. My shoulders touch the side of the small tunnel. There's not much room to excavate the rocks. Each time I push them behind me, my left shoulder screams. I'm thankful the rocks aren't very big. It's got to be ten a.m. by now in Chicago. My father will be opening the store.

At the bottom of the pile, I scrape the smaller pebbles away from the opening. My fingernails bleed as if I'm clawing my way out of a coffin. Thirty hours. I've been in darkness for thirty hours. It's early afternoon Chicago time. My father will be closing the store, going for lunch. Walking down Wabash with the L trains clacking overhead on his way to his favorite hot dog stand. He loves Chicago hot dogs.

My luck runs out. I can't move this rock. It's too big. It's too heavy. It won't budge. Probably more than a hundred pounds. It's the size of the tunnel I'm in. It's wedged its way between me and the light. I can't pull it back. I can't push it forward. My father will be back at the shop by now. It must be late afternoon. Time for his second pot of tea. Is he worried about me? Is he trying to call me? My phone is back at the hotel. I had told no one of my plan to enter this abandoned mine.

The saltwater rushes in, filling my tunnel. The rock is moving. It has no place to go but on top of me. I'm sorry, Father; I'm sorry I didn't listen to you. I'm sorry I'm not there to help you at the store. I'm sorry that you'll have to bury your only daughter.

I can feel the ground rumbling. The cork is going to blow. With every bit of my last strength, I try to push the cork out of the bottle, pushing my shoulder against it. I dig in with my heels. I push. It falls out, my eyes blinded by light. Five yards in front of me. The entrance of the mine. Sitting right in my path, I see that the muddy, brownish rock that held me captive is encrusted with crystals of alexandrite.

Chapter Two

My shoulder twinged as I reached across the counter and handed the ruby ring back to the eager woman standing in front of me. "It's not a Burmese ruby," I told her, standing up from my stool. My shoulder twinged again. Six months of rehab, and it still bothered me.

"My grandmother told me it was a genuine Burmese ruby. Look at that color; it's pigeon blood red. It's a beautiful stone. It's from the 1920s. It's a family heirloom," the woman argued with me.

I took the ring back and glanced at it again, not needing to take a second look. The three-carat ruby surrounded by two carats' worth of round diamonds was a nice-enough ring, but it wasn't an antique. And the ruby certainly wasn't a pigeon blood Burmese. "The ring and the diamonds are possibly from the 1920s, but the ruby is early to mid-1990s."

"Wait a minute. How can you tell that?" She interrupted me. Her face turned as red as the ruby.

"In the 1990s, the Mong Hsu mines produced lower-grade rubies that had a more bluish purple color. Gem labs in Thailand heat-treated the rubies to give them that Burmese pigeon blood color. They're nowhere near as valuable as a natural Burmese pigeon blood ruby," I told her.

"How can you tell the stone was heat-treated?"

"It's not uncommon. Many stones are heat-treated. In fact, ninety-five percent of rubies on the market are heat-treated to enhance their natural color. In this case, dealers take the bluish-colored stones and heat them to almost their melting point. This allows the aluminum oxide in the stone to reform, creating a new crystal structure. The chromium in the stone combines with different atoms, giving it a deep red hue. The borax-based chemicals used in the heat-treatment process turn rubies' natural inclusions glassy in appearance." I put the stone back under the microscope. "You can see the inclusions in the stone. These little breaks are glassy and smooth. A natural, untreated ruby's inclusions are more needlelike. This stone is a poor grade and was treated to imitate the pigeon blood color." I swung my microscope around so she could look through it to see what I was seeing. "I have a tray of true Burmese pigeon blood natural rubies if you want to see the difference."

"No thank you. I still think you're wrong." As she reached to grab the ring from my hand, our hands touched over it. A burst of energy shot up my arm. My shoulder ached.

"Your grandmother was Hungarian?" I asked.

"Yes, how did you know?"

"Jewish?"

"Why are you asking me these questions?" She grabbed the ring from my hand and stormed out. My head pounded.

As she reached for the door handle, my father, who was just about to enter through the other side, held the door open for her and nodded politely.

"Alexandra, what was that about?" he asked me, entering the store and watching her storm off through the large picture window.

"She's an idiot. I tried to explain the difference between heat-treated rubies and natural rubies. She didn't want to hear about it." I used a rag to scrub the fingerprints off the glass display case. I didn't look at my father.

"Alexandra, we've talked about this. You have to be nicer to the customers. We have a business." My father leaned on the counter that I had just cleaned.

"You know I'm not good behind the counter. I don't have your people skills." I couldn't look at him. My eyes scanned the prism of colors hidden in the cases—the lime-green peridots, the deep amethyst purple, the golden citrine. I was more comfortable with the stones in the cases than the people who walked in the door. My father knew that.

"You don't need people skills. Be polite and sell something," he said. "I have appointments all afternoon with some high-end buyers. I want to talk to you first. Come in the back with me."

I scanned the glass display cases that lined the perimeter of our small Wabash Avenue storefront—Kustodia Kollections. Located in the heart of jeweler's row in Chicago, my great-grandfather had opened it when he'd arrived here from Russia before the 1918 revolution. My grandfather had continued the business, and now it was my father's turn. I grew up in the store, but it was not my passion. Instead, my passion lay in finding the stones, hunting the world for these gems.

I followed my father into the small back room, which served as both a break room and his lapidary lab. His microscope, cutting, and setting tools were here. He, like his father and grandfather before him, was a master jeweler. In the far corner was our floor-to-ceiling vault, which held the most valuable stones and jewelry.

"Alexandra, sit down. I'll make us some tea," my father said.

I sat and watched my father, Peter Kustodia. A giant of a man, he delicately sipped the black tea. His hamlike hands made it appear as if he was playing with a child's tea set. His barrel chest and long black beard intimidated many customers when they first came to our store until they got to know him and realized what a gentle bear he is. I don't share his disposition. I have my mother's temper along with her long white-blond hair, sea-green eyes, and her curves. When I turned thirteen, I shot up to five feet ten inches, and the rest of my body filled in. I learned quickly how to keep the hormone-stricken boys at bay.

"Here, Alexandra." My father handed me a sugar cube.

I placed it in my mouth and sipped my tea through it. It's the Russian way. Or at least the old Russian way. Everything my father does is the Russian way, the pre-Soviet way.

"Alexandra, do you remember when you were a little girl, no more than five or six?" My father sat on the chair across from me, balancing the delicate teacup in his large hands. "Your mother took you to the Auditorium Theater to see the Joffrey Ballet."

"Yes, I remember."

"You remember how much you loved the *Nutcracker*. You begged us for ballet lessons."

"Father, I have two left feet. I tried for two long years. I couldn't do a pirouette." I remembered how proud I'd been of my little pale pink tutu and matching ballet slippers.

"Yes, but you never gave up, did you? Your mother was so proud of her little ballerina."

"I don't have mother's grace, her elegance. After she died, you and grandfather raised me like a son."

"Yes, I regret that now. I didn't know how to raise a daughter. I did the best I could."

"Father, why are we talking about this now?" I

downed my tea.

"I'm worried about you. You're twenty-six years old. You're single. You take too many chances."

"Is this about India?" Since I'd returned home, battered and bruised, my father constantly brought up my expedition.

"Yes, I warned you. I ordered you not to go. You knew the risk. Those mines are constantly flooding and dangerous. It's illegal to be there."

"But the payoff was worth it." My shoulder twinged again. I hid the pain from my father.

"The vault is filled with precious gems, enough to make all the jewelry we need for years. I want you to stay in the store. Work with me. I'll teach you how to polish and cut, how to create beautiful custom pieces like your grandfather and my grandfather did. They were artists."

"I would go nuts if I were cooped up here all day. I know it's what you love to do, but I can't sit and cut stones all day. I don't have the patience or the eye."

"Alexandra, you do have the eye. No one knows gems better than you."

"Yeah, rough stones. I know where and how to find them. I know what to look for. That's what I love to do. The alexandrite I brought back from India will easily yield a hundred carats, some single pieces as large as seven or eight carats. That's what we need to do. We need to do more hunting."

My father set his teacup down. "I have a buyer for that stone."

"How many carats?"

"He wants the whole piece, anything we can cut out of it."

"That's great. It can fund my next expedition. I've heard they've found sunset rubies in Pailin. I can take the money from the alexandrite and buy a large selection of rough, uncut rubies, maybe even go to the mine for the best selection." I felt my excitement build. It had been six months since India, and I was ready for my next find.

"This is what I'm talking about. I don't want you going to those third-world countries. They're dangerous, and you're a woman."

"I'm a woman? What's that supposed to mean?"

"It's dangerous for a woman in some of those countries."

"Father, I can take care of myself." As I spoke, I reached down and felt the nine-inch bench-made boot knife that I always carried. The streets of Chicago could be as dangerous as the streets of Cambodia.

My father put another sugar cube in his mouth and sipped his tea. "Yes, I know you're talented with a knife, but I don't want you traveling anymore."

"It's not your decision." I stood up. I left through the back door that led into the alley behind the store. The famous Chicago wind whipped through the alley and through my cotton sweater. I had walked out without grabbing my jacket. Though still early fall, I could already smell winter coming.

I headed home. My apartment is a short distance from Wabash, from the store. I needed to walk, to cool down. I arrived at my building, a high-rise named the Legacy in Millennium Park. I waved to Ron the doorman as I entered the front door and took the elevator up to the sixtieth floor. I opened the door to my condo and was greeted by Hunter, my beautiful black-and-white Borzoi. Trailing at his heels was Gem, my Russian Blue cat. I knelt down and hugged Hunter as Gem meandered through my legs, purring loudly. "Hi, guys! I'm home for a while. We'll go for a walk soon, Hunter."

I fed the impatient Gem and pulled a bottle of

vodka out of my freezer. I poured a big glass and sat on the couch overlooking the Chicago loop and Willis Tower. I felt very small and claustrophobic. I never felt that way in a mine or a cave or any hole in the ground. In Chicago, I was just one of millions, insignificant, like my condo, no different than the one across the hall, above me, or under me. I looked around the room at the black granite and stainless steel kitchen, the white walls, white modern furniture that came with my condo. I never bothered making it my own. It wasn't my home. I felt like a visitor, almost a thief who broke in. I sunk farther into the leather skin of the couch. The city wasn't the place for me.

I picked up the business card on my end table and flipped it back and forth between my fingers. It was time to make the call. I'd make my money back on the condo and then some, enough money to fund several expeditions. The first one would be Pailin, Cambodia, and sunset rubies. I called the management company of the Legacy. They'd offered to buy my condo. Now I was ready. Everything I needed I could put in a backpack except Gem and Hunter, but my grandfather loved them and they loved him. They stayed with him when I traveled— which was most of the year anyway.

I looked out the window again. Yes, the city was not the place for me. I don't thrive well around people. Gem jumped on my lap and nuzzled her head against me. Animals I understand. They're simple. No pretense. I poured another glass of vodka. The high tolerance was in my bloodline.

Hunter joined us on the couch, always quiet, always watching. Borzois are sight hounds, any peripheral movement will get Hunter going, but he allows Gem to move around freely because they were raised together. As I pet his soft fur, I wished I could bring Hunter with me on my next expedition, but I feared he wouldn't survive the journey. He's turning ten, which is old for a Borzoi. It makes me sad to think of my life without him in it. When he was younger, he traveled with me to Montana to hunt sapphires, to Arkansas to look for diamonds, and to the Carolinas for emeralds. I worried about taking him out of the country due to his sensitive nature and many countries' quarantine rules. I would have loved for him to see Russia, the motherland. I've been there twice as a young girl to visit the place where my great-grandfather started the family business. My father and grandfather wanted me to see it.

Putting my glass down, I walked to the door and grabbed Hunter's leash. He jumped off the couch, leaning against me while I put it on him. I shrugged into my black North Face jacket. We walked to the elevator, and I pressed the down button. My neighbor gave Hunter a wary look as he got off the elevator when it stopped on our floor. Many people were afraid of Hunter due to his size. I didn't tell them that my gentle dog was probably more afraid of them.

Stepping out into the early-evening air, Hunter and I strode along the walkway into Millennium Park. As the sun went down, the city lights came on. We stopped at the Bean, the giant mirrored sculpture that tourists flocked to. Hunter watched as people admired their reflections in the Bean. He also caught glimpses of the chipmunks playing in the surrounding bushes. I find the people interesting also as long as they keep their distance. I study them with a quiet curiosity.

When I'd journeyed to Ethiopia to search for opals, I traveled through several remote villages. Some of the children had never seen a white woman before, especially one with long white-blond hair and green eyes. They were fascinated. They wanted to touch me, to understand. Here I'm not a curiosity. I'm just one of the crowd except when I get glances from men especially married men looking over their shoulders as they walk along the path with their wives, studying me in the same way the children in Ethiopia studied me, wanting to touch me. Hunter scares off many of them. Maybe that's one of the reasons I love him so. I took his big pointy head in my hands, kissed his long nose, and rubbed his big, deep chest. "*Ya Tebya Lyublyu*," I whispered in his ear. "I love you."

We strolled back to our condo, Hunter pausing a few times to sniff. After getting off the elevator on the sixtieth floor, I unlocked my door and went in. "Gem!" I yelled out. She usually runs to the door when she hears the key. "Gem!" I called again. "Where are you?" Hunter seemed as upset as I was and took off to the bedroom where he found Gem hiding under the bed. I bent down and tried to coax her out. I could see she was shaking. "Kiska, come to me, Kiska." I talked softly using my pet name for kitty. She came out and I held her. I sat on the bed and rocked her. I turned to Hunter, who was still pacing and growling. "What has you so upset?" I asked him.

Hunter ignored me. He traveled around the room, smelling, stopping, and growling. Something wasn't right. "Hunter, what is it you smell?"

Hunter came over, laid on my feet, and let out a deep growl.

Chapter Three

Balancing my cup of coffee, I unlocked the front door to my father's shop and walked in. The door shut behind me, and I heard the click of the lock as it closed. I didn't see my father in the front, so I went to the back. He was sitting on his stool, the alexandrite in front of him, his magnifying eyeglass over his eye, its beam of light reflecting off the stones. He pulled it off and glanced up at me.

"Father, what are you doing?"

"Trying to figure out the cleavage line, the best place to cut the stone. There are several good angles. If we sacrifice the potential for smaller stones, I think we can get one twenty-carat stone."

"Is this about that customer you were telling me about?" I stood in front of him and stared at the stone. In this light, it was reflecting glimpses of a rich red, which would be more spectacular once cut. "How'd you find this customer?"

"I told my associates on Rodeo Drive that we had a spectacular specimen of alexandrite and to put out the word for a buyer before I cut it."

"Rodeo Drive? Who is this guy?"

"Some Hollywood movie star. His manager contacted my friend who contacted me. He's coming in this morning."

"Have you thought about using the money for Pailin?"

"We had this conversation, Alexandra; it's too dangerous. I don't want you traveling anymore."

"Too dangerous. Chicago's not dangerous?" I sat down on the stool next to him and put my hand on his leg.

The front door buzzer broke through our argument. We both turned to look at the monitors we kept in back. I recognized my father's customer right away in spite of his large hat and larger sunglasses, but the two men next to him were unfamiliar. My father ran to get the door and let them in. I followed him slowly to greet them.

"Welcome! Welcome!" My father held out his hand to shake theirs.

The first man, who was wearing a business suit, said. "I'm Andy Kinzel. I spoke with your friend, Seth, at Rodeo Jewelry. We talked on the phone."

"Yes, please come in," my father said.

"This is Jake," Andy said, pointing to the larger man. Looking at Jake, I realized his part in the trio. He was as big as my father. I could see the bulge of a gun underneath his expensive suit.

"And, of course, this is Tom Carter." The pint-sized action hero flashed a big grin as he pulled his sunglasses off, revealing his sapphire-blue eyes as though he thought he was a mystery. I was not impressed.

My father shook his hand. "Yes, of course; I've seen your movies. Please come. Let me bring the stone out. This is my daughter, Alexandra."

"Alex, just call me Alex."

Tom Carter shone his smile my way, shaking my hand, waiting for my reaction. He seemed disappointed that I had none.

They sat at the small table, which had several comfortable chairs. The table's surface had a built-in light. My father rushed into the back room and returned with the sixty-pound chunk of rock I'd risked my life for. He placed it in front of the two men. Jake stood by the front door.

"Doesn't look like much," Tom Carter said.

"These chunks of red stone are raw, natural alexandrite," my father said, turning the stone in different directions to show off the crystal encased inside. "Once they're cut and polished, they will look much different. They will be magnificent gems."

"Still looks like a hunk of rock to me," Tom Carter said.

"That hunk of rock is rare because of its scarcity," I said. "What makes a stone valuable is its perceived value based upon its scarcity and the level of difficulty obtaining it."

Tom Carter gave me a blank stare.

"It's like tulip mania in the 1600s. Peasants mortgaged their farms and went into debt all to obtain the scarce tulip bulbs. The tulip market burst when the town hosting the auction was infected with the bubonic plague. They lost everything."

"Still doesn't look like much. And it's red. I thought my manager said it was green," Tom Carter said.

I jumped in. "Alexandrite is one of the only stones that changes colors depending on the light. In daylight, it reflects green or bluish green, and in incandescent light like this it turns reddish. Alexandrite is part of the chrysoberyl family like emeralds. All chrysoberyls contain iron and titanium. Unlike other chrysoberyls, alexandrite also contains chromium, which is responsible for its color change. That very chemical composition makes alexandrite so scarce."

Tom Carter picked up the stone and studied it. He struggled to hold what my father had carried in one hand. "You're saying this is the best of the best. If so, we'll take it. That's why we're here. Our source told us this stone has been mined out. I want my girlfriend to have only the best of the best."

I jumped in again. "Actually, it's not the best of the best. The best specimens come from the Ural Mountains in Russia."

He put the stone down. "Why are we here then?" He glanced back at his manager, who had no answer.

"Those mines were depleted decades ago. There's no more Russian alexandrite to be found. This stone is the closest thing to it. It's from the same vein that runs from the two thousand five hundred miles of the Ural Mountains into India," my father said.

Tom Carter sat, examining the stone, turning it. "How many carats would this cut to?"

"We could make you a beautiful twenty-carat pendant."

"It's not going to be as beautiful as the Russian alexandrite, is it?"

"Nothing is," I said.

"Excuse me a minute." Tom Carter got up, grabbed his manager, and pulled him toward the door. They whispered quietly.

His manager came back to us. "Listen, there's been a misunderstanding. We're not interested in this stone anymore. Thank you for your time."

My father's face fell. Tom Carter donned his sunglasses and hat. Jake peeked out the door to make sure the coast was clear, Tom Carter watching behind him.

"Wait!" I yelled. I ran over to him. I stood nearly four inches taller, slouching a bit so as not to make him uncomfortable and to look into his eyes. "Your girlfriend wants an alexandrite?"

"She doesn't care about what stone. She wants a beautiful custom necklace to wear on the red carpet at the premiere of my new movie. She's been to every jeweler in New York and LA. It's all the same pieces that someone else has or will be wearing. She wanted something unique for her."

"The red carpet. How does she feel about a red gem?"

"She was excited about alexandrite," Tom Carter said.

"How does she feel about rubies?"

"She has rubies. She looked at rubies. They're not special."

"If you want the best of the best, what about the world's finest, rarest ruby, a sunset ruby? I can guarantee you that no one else walking down the carpet will be wearing a sunset ruby. Instead of a pendant with a twenty-carat alexandrite, what about a whole necklace full of hundreds of carats of perfectly matched rubies, the best in the world?" I asked.

"You have that? You have that piece here?" He took his sunglasses off.

"Alexandra!" My father interrupted. I held my hand up to stop him.

"No, but I can get it."

"Alexandra." My father interrupted again.

I gave him a pointed glance and went back to Tom Carter, slouching again, staring into his eyes. "I don't have it here, but I know where to get it. It's in Pailin, Cambodia. I can go there as your agent and bargain in the village for the stones, maybe even possibly go to the mines and dig it myself."

Tom Carter slouched down. He glanced back at his manager who shook his head "no." He turned back to me. "How long will this take?"

"I'll need to get the proper entry papers, book a flight, set up contacts. I know a lot of dealers in the area who can get me in front of the stones. It will probably take me about a month to get everything together."

"I don't have that kind of time. I need a necklace in six weeks."

"That's going to be expensive. I'll need at least thirty thousand dollars just for expenses plus the cost of the stones. On top of that, our commission is twenty percent of whatever we find. My father can cut them and have them ready in time."

Tom Carter thought for a moment. "The money's not the problem. Neither are the travel arrangements. My plane is at Midway, and I have people who can help with the entry papers we need."

"What do you mean *we*?" I stared at him.

"I'm coming with you."

"I don't think that would be a good idea. It's a dangerous area. The people I'll be dealing with aren't under government control."

"I've been around the world. I've shot movies in much more dangerous places. I think I can handle myself." He flashed his twenty-million-dollar smile. He held out his hand.

I didn't see his charm, but I saw my chance to find some amazing rubies, so I shook his hand. "Deal."

He stood up, walked toward the door, turned around. "I'll have everything you need in a couple of days. We'll be in contact. Thank you." He put his sunglasses back on. Jake, the bodyguard, opened the door, leading the men out.

My father stood still, staring at me, not understanding everything that had happened. "Alexandra, you're not doing this. We'll find another buyer for the alexandrite."

"Father, it's a chance to not only find some beautiful rubies but to make important connections in Hollywood and New York. It's a good opportunity for the business. Grandfather would agree." I knew the way to convince my father was to make it about business. "Your piece will be photographed on the red carpet. Millions of people will hear the name, Kustodia Kollections. You know how many people watch Tom Carter's movies?"

My father sat down behind the table and stared at the alexandrite. He couldn't argue with me. He knew I was right. "Father, this guy's a big shot movie star. He's going to have lots of security and connections. We'll be safe. We'll be in and out in four days. I won't take any chances."

"You mean like in India?"

"That was different. I was on my own."

My father stroked his beard. "We'll talk about this over dinner at your grandfather's on Sunday. He's making beef stroganoff."

"Father, I have to get ready."

"Your grandfather will want to see you before you leave."

"Okay," I said. I gave him a hug and kissed him just as the buzzer rang again.

"My next client is here." He shooed me away as he opened the door. His client, an elderly Gold Coast longtime customer, walked in. They sat at the table and reviewed designs for a new ring.

I went into the back room and called some of my contacts in Thailand. I'd need a bush pilot. I didn't mention to my dad or Tom Carter that the new mines were located in a part of the jungle run by drug cartels. That was a conversation I didn't want to have with either of them.

By the end of the day, I'd planned most of the trip except for hiring a bush pilot. Carter's people were working on logistics, including making hotel arrangements.

I sat at the table, staring at the rock encrusted with the alexandrite. The rock that had almost cost me my life. I ran my hand over the stone, touching the crystal encased in the muddy brown stone. My head ached, my shoulder twinged. I could taste saltwater. My shoulder screamed. The room grew dark. I was blind. My heart pounded. I couldn't catch my breath. I opened my mouth, but nothing came out. I felt a hand on my shoulder. I opened my eyes; my father was standing above me.

"Alexandra, what's wrong?"

I shook my head. "Nothing. Nothing. I'm just tired." I got up. I said goodbye to my father who was locking the valuable jewelry in the cases in the vault in the back room.

I headed back to my condo to meet the woman from the management company. She was waiting outside my door when I reached it.

"Linda Glidden, so nice to meet you," she said, reaching out her hand as she spoke. She looked nothing like I'd imagined from hearing her voice on the phone. Short and round and very perky, her blue blazer and blue polyester pants were stretched to their limits.

I shook her hand.

"I don't believe we've met. You moved in before I started working for the building," she said. "Can we go inside and talk?"

I opened the door. Hunter was already at attention, smelling Ms. Glidden in the hallway. Gem had taken off for one of her hiding places. "Friend," I said to Hunter, who relaxed and lay behind the couch.

"What a big dog," Linda said, stepping back when she saw him. "Is he friendly?"

"Not friendly but safe. You don't have to worry about him."

"Shall we sit? I need you to sign the listing papers."

I cleared all the old newspapers off the dining room table and made room for us. I sat at the head of the table. Linda sat across from me, rifling through her folder of papers. "Ms. Kustodia, is that how you pronounce it? Kustodia?"

"Yes."

"I have very good news for you. Condos on this floor have gone up substantially in the past year. I think you'll make a tidy little profit."

"I'm in no hurry, so whatever you think we should list it for."

"The management company for the building would be glad to buy it from you. They'd either sell it or lease it so you don't have to worry about the mess of showing or listing the property yourself. We could even do a buyback for you to give you more time if you need to find another home."

"I'm going to be out of the country for a while. I'm not worried about finding another home."

She showed me their offer, and I signed the papers.

Chapter Four

At precisely four p.m., I walked into Russian Tea Time on Adams Street, located just a few blocks from our store. Minna didn't like me or anyone to be late. She was already sitting at her booth, the one reserved just for her. I stopped to observe her for a moment as people quietly came up, showed their respect, some just nodding, others bending down and whispering to her. I waited until the procession went by.

This was not unusual, especially in the Chicago Russian community. Minna was what the Russian community calls a *silovik* or what Americans would call a person of influence. If you needed something done, Minna would be the person to go to. She was involved in many local Russian foundations and had great political pull both in Chicago and back in Russia.

She'd been given the place of honor—the booth overlooking the street—as she liked to observe the passersby, commenting on their fashion as they went about their day. Minna was always dressed elegantly. Today she was wearing her classic black wool suit. Wrapped twice around her neck was her statement piece, an ornate, handcrafted gold chain with diamond stations. She had sewn it into her skirt hem when she'd escaped from Nazi Germany. On her ring finger, she wore a five-carat diamond, a souvenir from one of her many gem-hunting expeditions. The ring fit loosely as her finger had shrunk with age. Each year brought her closer to the ground until one day I imagined she would just disappear. But that day was far from this day. Longevity ran in her family as did her quick wit. Even at eighty years old, Minna could still hold her own.

At her side was her gold-handled walking stick decorated with a large green tourmaline that she'd mined herself when she was about my age. She sat quietly watching me enter the room—neither smiling nor frowning—just watching. I checked my watch to make sure I wasn't late. I wasn't. I walked up to her and kissed her paper-thin cheek. I sat across from her in the booth.

"Minna, thank you so much for meeting me on such short notice," I said.

"What else does an old woman have to do?" she replied, sipping her black Darjeeling tea.

I poured myself a cup from the teapot on the table.

Minna waved to the waiter who rushed over. "Yes, Minna?" he asked with a polite nod of his head.

"You can bring our sandwiches now," she commanded.

The waiter walked away.

"Minna, I wanted to talk to you," I said.

"Not until we eat," she replied.

We sat in silence while the waiter brought over a three-tier tray filled with small bites, including salmon-and-cream-cheese sandwiches with dill, spring crepes, potato latkes, and mushroom quiche. He set it on the table and refilled our teacups. Minna nibbled at the edge of a sandwich and then wiped the corners of her mouth with the tip of her napkin as though notifying all that she was done with her meal. I'd already eaten five sandwiches.

"Now we talk," she said, putting her napkin back in her lap.

"I need your help," I said. "One of my sources told

me there's a new find of sunset rubies outside Pailin. I'm planning a buying trip to Cambodia. I've called all my contacts that I know in Burma. Between the government restrictions and the warlords, I haven't been able to get safe passage out of the city to the mines. I was hoping you might have some connections."

Minna cradled her teacup and studied me. She sat quietly and took some loose leaf tea out of her purse, sprinkling it carefully into her cup. She closed her eyes as the tea seeped. Then she sipped the tea with her left hand. Holding the teacup in both hands, she gave it three good swirls and gently dumped out the remaining liquid onto her saucer. She breathed in three times and turned the cup back upright. Then she stared at the remaining leaves. This wasn't the first time I'd seen her read tea leaves. Occasionally she would entertain us with readings at family parties and celebrations. It always made me nervous. Not that I believe in such things, but the fact that *she* did and because I *admired* her, it made me nervous.

"Alexandra, I don't think it's a very good idea for you to travel at this time," she finally said. "Pailin is a very volatile, dangerous place, and to go outside of Pailin is even more dangerous."

"Minna, I'm going. My trip is already scheduled. If you can't help me, I can make my own arrangements." I stood up.

She grabbed my arm and pulled me back down. She took a fountain pen out of her purse and scribbled something on a napkin. She handed it to me and closed her hand around mine. "This man is a trusted friend. He's a bush pilot. He knows the area. He knows how to handle authorities and the drug lords. I don't think you should go, but I know you're going anyway. Contact this man and tell him I sent you."

I kissed Minna on the cheek. "Thank you," I whispered, slipping the piece of paper in my pocket.

"I'll see you at Sunday dinner," Minna said.

I wrapped my coat around me. I felt a sudden chill.

Chapter Five

My Uber driver dropped me in front of the large red stone farmhouse where my grandfather lived in the near west suburb of Oak Park. My grandmother had made him move out of the city when my father was young. After she died, he'd insisted on remaining in the house. Holding Hunter's leash and carrying Gem's cage, I walked up the long driveway and knocked on the front door. My grandfather had offered to watch my companions while I was away. He opened the door. He was wearing his Bermuda shorts, high black socks, and a red long-sleeve flannel shirt. This was his standard uniform. I'd only seen him wear a suit once—at my grandmother's funeral.

"Alexandra!" he exclaimed, pulling me into his big arms. He kissed me on each cheek, and then he bent down to pet Hunter.

A bear of a man like my father, he was nearly eighty years old, and he could still lift me off the ground. I followed him into the house and turned right toward the living room. The furniture hadn't been updated since the 1960s when they'd moved into the house. My father was sitting on the avocado-green fabric couch, finishing his first glass of vodka and leafing through an old issue of *National Geographic*. He rose to kiss me.

As I sat in the wing-back chair by the fireplace, my grandfather, Alexander, whom I was named after, handed me a glass of vodka. No one left his house hungry or sober. "Alexandra, your father told me you plan to travel to Cambodia." My grandfather sat in the chair across from mine. "I've heard about the sunset rubies. I wish I could go with you."

My father gave us both a pointed look. "It's too dangerous. She should not go," he said, putting the magazine down and pacing around the room.

"That's what I told *you* about the Ural Mountains. Did you listen? No. Did you find many valuable stones? Yes. I was wrong then, and you're wrong now. We're Kustodias; this is what we do."

I interrupted them both. "I spoke to Minna. She's connected me with a bush pilot who knows the area. Tom Carter's security team is coming with us. We've got a private jet that's flying us into Thailand and plenty of money to bribe our way past the authorities and the drug lords."

"See, Peter, the girl knows what she's doing. She'll be fine. And the sunset ruby, I've only seen a few. If this find is true, then the reward is worth the risk." My grandfather paused. "Why is this Tom Carter coming with you?"

"He wants to pick the stones out personally for his girlfriend," my father said.

"He thinks he's a real-life action hero. I think he wants to feel the rush, the danger of Cambodia," I said.

"You mind him. Don't let his ego get in your way," my grandfather said.

"Grandfather, this is my expedition. I'll set the ground rules," I told him.

There was a knock at the door. Hunter jumped up from his spot by the fire and beat my grandfather to the door. "Sit, boy!" my grandfather commanded Hunter. He opened the door, and Minna walked in, handing my grandfather a bottle of Stoli.

She stood quietly and then cleared her throat. My

grandfather took her coat off her and hung it on the hall tree. Minna turned and nodded at him.

My father jumped up to greet her. "Minna, so nice to see you," he said, kissing both her cheeks.

"Peter," she replied.

Hunter stood watching. I motioned for him to go lay down. He went back to his spot by the fire. I walked over, kissed Minna's cheeks. "Nice to see you again."

"Please come in." My grandfather took Minna's arm and walked her to the chair by the fireplace.

"The stroganoff smells good, Alexander," Minna said.

"I think it's about ready. We can go sit at the table." My grandfather stood up.

"Let's talk first," Minna said.

My father and grandfather both sat on the couch next to me. "I'm sure Alexandra has told you I'm concerned about her traveling to Pailin. I've made some phone calls, and the stories of the sunset rubies are true. If it were not for my obligations here in Chicago, I would go with her," Minna said. "I think it's a good opportunity for your store. I've given Alexandra the name of a guide who I trust and have used many times."

"Minna, I appreciate your helping the family out," my father said. "I had this conversation with Alexandra after India. I want her to help at the store more and travel less."

Minna stood up. "I'm hungry. It's time to eat." With those words, the conversation was over.

My grandfather led us into the small dining room. It hadn't changed since my grandmother was alive. The table was set with her fine Bavarian china, one of the few possessions she'd brought with her from Russia. My grandfather ran into the kitchen. My father pulled out Minna's chair, sitting her at the corner next to my grandfather. I sat down across from her so we could talk. Minna pounded the table. "Up! What are you doing, girl?"

I got up and sat at the end. Minna looked over at my father. "Haven't you taught Alexandra any of the Russian traditions?"

"It's not really a tradition; it's a superstition which I don't believe in," I said.

"Tradition, superstition—makes no difference. Unmarried women should never sit at the corner of the table. In the old days, only old maids and peasant women were placed at the lowest place of honor at the table. If an unmarried woman sits in that place, they won't be married for seven years," Minna said.

I thought to myself that wouldn't be so bad.

My grandfather brought two steaming bowls from the kitchen—one filled with hot buttered noodles and the second with tender pieces of beef, smothered with a cream sauce and overflowing with mushrooms. We filled our plates and ate silently.

Hunter sat transfixed, staring at my grandfather, waiting for any movement of his hand.

"Talk to your granddaughter. She's reckless. She should be married, working in the store, not traveling the world," my father said.

"Alexandra can take care of herself. We've taught her well," my grandfather replied, standing. He left the room and came back a few minutes later, carrying a rifle. He placed it in front of me.

I studied it. "Mosin Nagant M91?" I said out loud, checking the chamber and unlocking the bolt. I tried the lever action, which was smooth as I knew it would be. I could smell the grease, the oil. The rifle was as old as my grandfather and just as sturdy and reliable.

"Alexandra, you keep this by your bed," my grandfather said. "You hear any noise, you shoot, then you ask questions. Understand?"

I half thought of pulling the Glock nine millimeter from my purse to reassure him, but I thought better of it. Instead, I changed the subject, not wanting to continue this discussion. "Grandfather, a perfect sunset ruby the size of my fingernail can be worth hundreds of thousands of dollars if it's heat-treated correctly. Will you teach me your secret?" I asked. For years, I'd tried to convince him to trust me with the family process of heat-treating colored stones. He had always said it wasn't time.

Grandfather sat back in his chair. I could hear it creak. He stroked his thick, long white beard. He took his pipe out of his pocket and packed it with tobacco. "It takes years to learn the proper way to treat a ruby. One mistake and the stone is ruined. The process hasn't changed since I was a little boy and my father taught me. Even with all the new chemicals, lasers and other technology, the old way is still best. You bring home the stones, and we'll do it together. I'll teach you."

I inhaled deeply. I loved the smell of my grandfather's tobacco. My father preferred cigarettes, but there was something about a freshly packed bowl. When I was little, no more than nine or ten, I snuck into my grandfather's den and smoked one of his pipes. It made me nauseous. When my grandfather caught me, I was so sick he didn't have the heart to punish me. Instead, he laughed his loud roar of a laugh. "Malenkaya," he said, his nickname for me. It means *little one* in Russian. "You're too young to smoke a pipe. When you're older, I'll teach you." I still didn't smoke in front of my father.

We finished our tea and apricot kolacky covered

with powdered sugar. We went back into the living room, and my grandfather threw logs on the fire. The wind rustled the leaves about on the front porch, dancing against the large bay window. The nights were getting colder, yet my grandfather rarely wore long pants. He was always warm. It was his Russian blood. The fire was more for ambiance, more for me. We talked about books, about the troubles in the Ukraine, as my grandfather called them.

And then I asked him to tell me the story he'd told me my whole life. The story about the old days and my great-grandfather who was a renowned jewelry maker. He was an artisan commissioned by all the members of the court of imperial Russia. Most of his work hadn't survived the revolution. My grandfather on his travels had scoured shops for pieces bearing his father's mark—our family crest, a wolf's head. He'd found a few small pieces, but most had been confiscated by the Bolsheviks.

He began the story. "When I was a boy, your great-grandfather took me back to his village by the Ural Mountains to show me where he used to mine alexandrite. He told me that when he was a jeweler to the imperial court, a young Grand Duke commissioned him to make a special necklace for a beautiful woman. My father spent two weeks in the mines searching for enough alexandrite to make a perfect infinity necklace. My father cut the stones perfectly, each one an exact match. When he was done, there were fifty perfect two-carat stones. On the back of the stones, the Grand Duke had him engrave a secret message for his beloved. Their love was a secret because she was married to a very powerful general. The necklace's secret message was only visible by candlelight when the stones turned from green to red. The Grand Duke planned to take her away from the general. She was only to wear the necklace the night of their escape, but she couldn't resist the beauty of it and one day placed it around her neck. When the general saw her wearing the necklace, he placed his hands around her neck. That next day, soldiers appeared at my father's door holding the necklace, confronting my father. My father had signed it as he did all his work with our family crest. My father would not give up the Grand Duke's name. He felt it a sacred oath. They beat him. He still would not give up the name. If it were not for the czar himself who favored my father's craftsmanship, my father would have been killed. Even though the czar saved his life, he still felt he was in constant danger from the general, so he decided to come to America. My father finally settled in Chicago and opened the store. No more than a year later, the Romanovs were assassinated. If he had never left Russia, I never would have been born and you wouldn't be sitting here listening. Neither one of you."

I watched my father as he listened to my grandfather. He enjoyed the stories as much as I did. Minna had heard this story many times and didn't seem as interested. She sipped her glass of Stoli and watched the crackling fire. I couldn't tell what she was thinking. Minna was very good at reading people and very good at keeping people from reading her.

It was nearly midnight, and the vodka and stroganoff were making me tired. I sat and listened as my father and grandfather exchanged stories. I stroked Gem, who was sitting on my lap. Hunter was sound asleep by the fire. I would miss my companions, but I knew they'd be well taken care of. I'd seen my grandfather sneak Hunter the leftover stroganoff. I gave a big yawn.

Grandfather stopped talking. "Alexandra, get to bed."

"I still have to finish packing at home."

"You can do that in the morning. Stay here tonight, and I'll drive you home in the morning," my grandfather said.

The thought of sleeping in my old feather bed with Hunter and Gem wrapped around me was a pleasant one. I did not bother arguing. I kissed them both goodnight and whispered to Minna, "Thank you," as I kissed her cheeks. Hunter jumped up and followed me upstairs, Gem right behind. I stared out the window of my childhood bedroom. It looked into the backyard and into the house next door where my friend, Lori Lloyd, used to live. I hadn't thought of her in years. We hadn't kept in touch after she'd moved to Florida. I wrote her name on the frost in the window like we used to do as little girls. Winter was coming but not where I'd be going. I got under the down blankets. Hunter lay on my feet, Gem on the pillow next to me, purring loudly. It had been a long time since I'd heard another heartbeat next to mine other than Gem and Hunter. I drifted off, listening to their heartbeats.

I woke up to the sound of my father yelling in the hallway. I checked my watch. It was two a.m. My bedroom door burst open. I sat up and stared at my father's disheveled hair. "What is it?" I asked him.

"Someone broke into the store."

"What are you talking about?"

My father held up his iPhone. "The silent alarm has been activated."

I cleared my eyes and walked over so I could see the monitor feed from his phone. I couldn't make out the man's face. We watched as he smashed the display cases with a hammer.

"The police are on their way. We have to go," my father said.

My grandfather ran up to us carrying an AK-47. My father stopped him. "Leave the gun. The police will be there by the time we get there."

I threw on my black leather coat and boots and slipped my knife back into my boot. We piled into my grandfather's Mercedes 450. Hunter and I sat in the back. My grandfather and father spoke in Russian to each other. I could only understand half of what they were saying. I wasn't fluent in Russian. The whole time we drove, my father watched on the phone as the intruder smashed one case after another. He turned around and showed me his phone.

"He's not taking anything. He's smashing all the cases, but he's not taking anything."

While my grandfather drove a hundred miles an hour down the Eisenhower, my father and I continued to watch the destruction of the jewelry cases. Then we saw the intruder enter the back room. He took a blowtorch from his bag, fired it up, and started cutting into the safe.

"That torch will never cut through," my father said.

By the time we arrived at the store, nine Chicago police cars were scattered out front, blocking off the street. My father jumped out of the car, barely waiting for my grandfather to apply the brakes. He ran toward the entrance, which was blocked by a uniformed officer. "My store!" he said.

I could hear the officer tell my father he'd have to wait outside while the detectives and the crime unit finished. I told Hunter to wait in the car, and I joined my father and grandfather.

"We have to wait for the detective in charge," my father said.

By the time the store was secured, the sun was rising, shining through the overhead L tracks. The detective let us into the store, asking us to take an inventory of any missing items, however, there didn't appear to be any. Whatever the robber had been looking for, he didn't find it. The hundred-year-old safe was barely scratched by the blowtorch. There must not have been enough time for him to get what he came for.

"Father, I don't understand. There had to be tens of thousands of dollars worth of jewels in the cases. Why wouldn't he take anything?" I asked.

"He knew the real money was in the safe," my father replied.

"Still, why not grab what you can?" I said. It made no sense to me.

My grandfather sank down onto one of the wooden jeweler stools. He shook his head, lowering his face into his hands. "All these years never a break-in."

I stood and looked around at all the broken glass, trying to make sense of what had happened. The building is a fortress, steel and brick, unbreakable windows. Somehow the thief was able to get in. The front door wasn't busted. According to the police detective, the intruder used a special key to enter. I reached for the broom and started sweeping.

"Come upstairs. I'll make breakfast," my father said. "Eat first. Then we'll clean up." My father waved at me to follow him upstairs to his apartment, which was only accessible from the back room. I followed him up. When we got to the top of the stairs, my father went to unlock the door, and it swung open. I pulled my knife out of my boot. My father pulled the nine millimeter from his back pocket. His small apartment had been torn apart, paintings hung off the wall, the couch was ripped up, the coffee table was flipped over, desk drawers balanced on their ends. Papers were scattered across the floor.

"Father, we have to call the detective back," I said.

"No," he said. "There's nothing they can do here. I don't want to involve the police."

In the old days, my father skirted the line of the law, occasionally dealing in black market gems. I never asked where some of his stones came from, and he never volunteered the information.

We cleaned up his apartment and made coffee. My father brought out black bread and jam. We sat in silence and ate. Hunter sniffed around the apartment, growling.

My father was the first to speak. "Our insurance will cover all the damage. Most important, he wasn't able to break into the safe."

"And no one was hurt," I added.

My grandfather kept shaking his head over and over. "After all this time, why now? Did he know about the alexandrite? You put the word out?" He pointed to my father.

"Just to trusted jewelers who we've done business with in the past," my father said.

I checked my watch. It was almost nine a.m. "I have to pick up my gear and get to Midway. I'm supposed to meet Tom Carter at eleven a.m."

"I'll drive you," my grandfather said.

Chapter Six

My grandfather dropped me outside the small office located near the private jet area of Midway Airport on Chicago's south side. I showed my passport to the receptionist, who checked it against her list. The small VIP office is located next to the hangar that houses private jets used by corporate executives and millionaires. A few moments later, Tom Carter, accompanied by his bodyguard and a young woman, sauntered up. He flashed his twenty-million-dollar smile at the receptionist and pulled his passport out of his back pocket. "No need, Mr. Carter; I'd recognize you anywhere," she said.

He took off his sunglasses, and his smile grew larger. The receptionist smiled back.

"We can board now if you're ready," the pilot said, stepping off the Gulfstream G550.

"Wait! We're waiting on a couple more passengers," Tom Carter said. As he spoke, a white panel van pulled up. Two men and a woman piled out, opening the back door of the van and taking out cameras and boom mics. Tom turned to the young woman and said, "Regina, I'd like to get some shots before we take off. Maybe something with me talking to the pilot, and also I want to shoot some footage of my guide. Let me introduce you." He waved me over to him. "Alex, this is my personal assistant, Regina. She'll be coordinating the documentary, and I'll be directing. The POV will be from my viewpoint."

I shook Regina's hand. "I'm Alex. Carter, what

are you talking about?"

He smiled again and took my arm. He walked me over to the plane. "I had this idea. Originally, I was going to shoot some footage to show my girlfriend— Cynthia is her name, by the way. I wanted to show her how I found the rubies. Then I started talking to my production company. We all agreed this would be a great opportunity for a doc, help promote the new movie."

"I didn't make arrangements for all these people. We're going to be flying out of Thailand into Cambodia in a small Cessna." I crossed my arms over my chest.

"Order two." Carter shrugged off my concern as if he was used to getting what he wanted.

"It doesn't quite work that way. There are a lot of flight restrictions. We're flying under the radar to begin with. Now you're bringing a Hollywood film crew."

He thought for a moment. "How about this? We'll shoot it big production going into Thailand, and then when we fly out, I'll use GoPro to really catch the action. Like Spielberg with *Saving Private Ryan*. I want it raw, natural, like a reality show." He paused. "Wait, that's what we'll call it—*Tom Carter's Reality.*"

I sighed and held my tongue. The whole time he spoke, Regina took notes. I could tell she was trying to capture every word. The documentary crew boarded the plane. I didn't know how to respond. At that moment, I just wanted to get to Thailand.

I followed everyone aboard the plane except for Jake who waited until Tom Carter was safely aboard. I stopped Jake as he went to sit across from me. "You know we can't take all these people," I told him.

"I wanted to bring a larger security team, but Tom

wanted to bring the film crew," Jake said.

I reclined back in the white leather seat. I was not used to this luxury. The thirty-two-inch TV was playing Carter's last movie. I hadn't seen it and didn't plan on watching it. A flight attendant greeted us and held out glasses of whiskey. Carter downed the glass. I declined and settled in for the twelve-hour flight.

During the flight, Carter flirted with the attractive, young flight attendant; her constant giggles made my head ache. I can't suffer stupid women. I put on my noise-canceling headphones to drown out her giggles. I pulled out my laptop and continued my research on recent finds in the area. Minna had given me a map of where she thought the mine would be located. I was familiar with the general area outside of Pailin but had never traveled to the Cardamom Mountains because the gems weren't worth the risk until now. As I fell asleep, I felt someone plop down next to me, grabbing my leg.

I opened one eye and saw Carter smiling, watching himself on the TV and me at the same time. "We shot that one in Columbia. Did you see it?"

I opened my other eye. "I don't see many movies."

"Not a fan, I get it." Carter nodded his head. "We were in the Columbian jungles for twelve weeks. At one hundred degrees, one hundred percent humidity. Air conditioner in my trailer only worked half the time."

"You realize there's no air-conditioning where we're going?"

"Of course I understand that." He nodded. "So tell me a little bit about Alex and your gem hunting. How'd you get started?" I sat up in my seat. Carter waved over the cameraman. I looked over, surprised. "Pretend, it's not there," Carter said. "Tell me about

Alex."

"I don't know anything different. It's a family business. It goes all the way back to my three-time great-grandfather. He made jewelry for Catherine the Great."

"She was great in that movie, *On Golden Pond*."

"No, that's Katherine Hepburn. Catherine the Great was empress of Russia in the 1700s. My great-grandfather made jewelry for the imperial court, Czar Nicholas. We've had our store in Chicago for almost a hundred years."

"What about you? Why travel around the world looking for precious gems?"

"It's my job," I said. I was already tired of his documentary.

Carter waved off the cameraman. "Listen, if we're going to make this work, you're going to have to open up a little. We have to see your passion."

"You hired me to find sunset rubies, and that's what I'm going to do. I didn't sign on for a movie."

He put his hand on my leg. "We'll work on it." He left my seat and went back to the flight attendant. I watched as the two of them snuck into the lavatory and closed the door behind them. I could hear giggles and moans from behind the closed door.

I put my headphones back on, turned John Hiatt up, closed my eyes, and drifted to sleep listening to "Buffalo River Home," his song about the pursuit of fruitless endeavors. When I woke, the pilot was landing on the tarmac in Bangkok.

After the plane cleared customs, we stepped off into the hot, humid air. Rain was pouring down. Carter's assistant held an umbrella over his head. I pulled up the hood of my sweatshirt. Two cars were waiting for us, and we headed to the Mandarin Oriental Hotel along the Chao Phraya River.

After we entered the hotel, Carter turned and looked at me. "What now?" he asked, the documentary crew filming over his shoulder.

"We'll be flying out in the morning. I'm meeting with our guide tonight. He'll take us into Pailin. From there, we'll take a jeep to the mines," I said.

"What about tonight? What will we do tonight?" Carter asked while his assistant checked us in.

"I'm handling the rest of the travel arrangements. You don't have to worry about that." I balanced my backpack on my shoulder.

He turned to the concierge. "What do we do for fun around here?"

The concierge beamed at him, bowed and said, "This is Bangkok. You can pretty much name your fun, Mr. Carter. Yes, I loved your last movie."

As we spoke, the flight attendant walked up behind Carter and put her arms around him. Carter turned to me. "We'll meet up later." He took off with the flight attendant.

Shaking my head, I went to the elevator and up to my room. I rested for a brief while before going downstairs to wait for Erik Helmstrom, Minna's contact. On the way, I knocked on Carter's door. I wanted to make sure he was in safe for the night. I knocked louder and then louder. No answer. "Damn."

I stopped at the concierge desk. "Can you ring Mr. Carter's room? He's not answering."

He smiled pleasantly at me. "Ms. Kustodia." He knelt close and whispered, "If you are referring to Mr. Carter, his room is reserved under his alias, Mr. Tomkat."

I stood silent, giving him a frustrated look. "Can you ring Mr. Tomkat's room?"

He continued whispering. "Mr. Tomkat—I mean, Mr. Carter—is not in his room. He left an hour ago."

"Where'd he go?"

"He asked about nightclubs, and I told him to try the Bamboo Room in the hotel. It's very nice, but it was not what he was looking for. He wanted the authentic Thai experience. I sent him to the Ka-Po district. To the Happiness Club."

"Happiness Club? What's that?"

"It's for American tourists who want to have an authentic Thai experience. Not everyone's taste. Mr. Carter seemed very excited."

I got directions and headed to the Happiness Club. It was nine p.m., and I still hadn't heard from Erik. I followed the backstreets to the Ka-Po district, avoiding the street hawkers selling everything from bootleg DVDs to knockoff jewelry. Some tried to entice me with rough stones, but I've learned not to buy in this area. On my walk, I had noticed the broken stoplights. A sign that the locals had crushed the glass with poor quality stones creating composites to attract unsuspecting tourists.

I reached a small warehouse where I could hear the techno dance music pumping. The only thing I hated more than cheap knockoff gems was Eurotrash and techno music. I was surprised to see a line waiting to get in. I walked up to the bouncer holding the velvet rope shutting off the front door. He put his big hand up to stop me from entering. He looked me up and down and then he looked at the line of tourists dressed in sequined miniskirts, colorful leggings and high, high heels. I was wearing baggy jeans, a T-shirt, and my Timberlands. He simply looked me over again and said, "No."

"I have a friend inside—a very important friend. I need to get in touch with him. Tom Carter."

He shook his head again. "No." He clicked his wireless Bluetooth and spoke in Thai.

I spoke back in Thai. "I know Mr. Carter's in there. Get a message to him that Alexandra Kustodia is in front. He'll want me to come in."

He stared at me again and shook his head "no." I walked the few blocks back to the open market. I went past the trays full of fresh crickets and beetles until I found the dress shop I'd passed on the way to the club. Hanging in the window was a green silk Thai dress. I grabbed it and ran to the small dressing room. I tried it on, eyeing myself in the full-length mirror. The slit up the side went up to my hip—not what I'd ever wear. Not what I wanted to wear. I grabbed a pair of black high heels and a silk green garter belt to hold my six-inch blade. I paid the woman and asked her to send my other clothes to the hotel.

Heading back to the club, I heard a group of Chinese businessmen whistling and speaking in Mandarin. My reply in Mandarin was "No way in hell, buddy," or that's what it meant loosely translated.

I returned to the club, and the line was longer than when I left. It was nearly ten p.m. I didn't have time to waste. I spoke to the doorman in Thai. "I've got a hundred dollars American if you let me in right now and a hundred when I walk back out."

He looked me over this time with a bit of a smile. The dress didn't allow room for a bra, and I'm not built to go without one. I don't usually feel self-conscious because I don't care what people think of me. But I hate that look. That look in a man's eye that says I'm here for his pleasure.

He unclipped the velvet rope, opened the door, and led me in. It sounded like the same song was playing, but I couldn't tell the difference except it was louder and playing in my head. The room was full of businessmen types, American tourists, locals, Eurotrash. It was a cheap version of Studio 54. All retro 70s sparkly disco dresses and glittery high heels. I couldn't tell the prostitutes from the tourists. They were all dressed the same. I made my way through the crowd, pushing away the hands grabbing me as I passed them. As I crossed the dance floor, I could see the VIP room on the second floor. Holding court was Mr. Tom Carter, enjoying his bottle service and Thai prostitutes. His security/bodyguard was passed out on the couch next to him.

Carter was throwing hundred-dollar bills, making it rain. When he saw me, he jumped up. "Alex, you're here! Come sit down. Have a drink." He pushed a champagne glass into my hand and filled it to overflowing with Dom. He grabbed a waitress and stuck some hundred-dollar bills in her sequined bustier. "Bring more bottles!" He slapped her on the backside as she walked away. Then he fell to the floor.

I picked him up and flung him onto the couch. I took the bottle of Dom out of the ice bucket and poured the entire bucket of ice water over his head. He jumped up, shook his head like a dog, and howled.

"That's what I'm talking about!" He screamed and started dancing.

I grabbed him by his soaked black T-shirt. "Listen!" I screamed over the noise. "You have to stop throwing money around. You're enough of a target just being who you are."

"Jake's got my back." He glanced over at the big six-foot-eight ex-wrestler who wouldn't get anyone's back tonight. I didn't even know if he'd make it to the hotel.

"We gotta get out of here now. I have to meet our

guide, and you have to get back to the hotel!" I shouted at him.

He eyed his Patek Philippe watch, worth more than I'll make in a lifetime. "It's early. Why don't you have some fun? Why don't you lighten up a bit?"

As I stood arguing with him, someone bumped into him, knocking him to the ground. Two men stood over him, speaking in Thai. They were saying, "Grab his watch." As the first man reached down to grab him, I hit him with the champagne bottle. The other man pulled out a knife and sliced at me. I jumped back, avoiding being cut. I pulled my knife out and sliced his arm. He dropped his knife and grabbed his friend. They took off. Tom Carter was under the glass cocktail table, watching. I pulled him out. "We're going now," I said. This time he didn't argue. Then I felt the bottle smash the back of my head, and I was out.

When I came to, my skull was throbbing and I reached up to touch clumps of sticky blood. I pulled a couple of chunks of glass out of my hair, then sat up on the leather couch. I was in a small office. Cases of wine were stacked up against one wall, and a desk with a computer and chair sat near the other. I stood and felt woozy, then quickly caught myself. I reached for the door handle, but it was locked. I reached for my knife. It was gone. I sat back down on the couch, held my face in my hands, rubbing my temples. A short while later, I heard the click of the door lock. It opened and a small Thai man in a shiny silk suit came in, carrying an ice bag. He walked over and handed me the bag, which I put on the back of my head. "Thanks, you're quite helpful."

He sat behind the desk. "Ms. Kustodia," he said in broken English. "Do you know who I am?"

I did not have an answer.

"We try to avoid trouble like yours in my club. It's not good for business. Your friend, Mr. Carter, is good for business. He makes people happy. They drink more alcohol. That makes me happy, but he also can be a problem, can't he?"

"What are you getting at?"

"There are elements in Thailand. Elements right here in the club that I have no control of. Men who may want to harm Mr. Carter, steal from him, maybe even kidnap him."

"Where's Carter?" I asked, standing up.

"Oh, Mr. Carter is quite safe, and that is the point of our conversation. It costs a lot of money to keep a man like Mr. Carter safe."

"How much do you want?" I asked.

The man did some calculations in his head. Then he pulled a calculator the size of an iPad out of his desk drawer, punched some numbers, and turned it around so I could see it.

"Fifty thousand dollars?" I said out loud. "You want me to pay you fifty thousand to protect Carter in your club?"

"I think that's fair. We've been taking care of him for you. He's a very big Hollywood movie star who makes movies seen by millions around the world."

"I've got ten thousand in the safe at the hotel. Let me go. I'll bring it back."

He walked out from behind the desk. He pushed my hair away from my face, wrapping it around my ear. "You're a very beautiful woman. Mr. Carter's very lucky." He glanced at his watch, which appeared to be the Patek that Carter had been wearing earlier. "It's two a.m. Be back in an hour. I charge by the hour."

I dropped the ice bag on the floor and staggered out of the club. I went back to the hotel. Up in my room, I opened the safe and counted out ten thousand dollars. I looked at myself in the mirror. I didn't have time to change. I headed down the elevator. Entering the lobby, I went to the Bamboo Room Bar. I was late to meet our guide, Erik Helmstrom. Its elegant décor was a far cry from the bar I'd just left. Thankfully, the only music playing was easy listening from the piano player singing some Sam Smith song. Somebody left somebody.

I sank into one of the comfortable chairs and ordered a vodka clean double. I didn't know what Erik looked like. Minna had only given me his name. I'd never spoken to him, only texted. I was the only five-foot-eleven iridescently white woman with long white-blond hair in the Bamboo Room, maybe in the hotel, maybe in all of Bangkok. I knew that he would recognize me. I stood out even more wearing the silk call girl evening gown and with the blood in my hair. If my father or grandfather saw me now, I could imagine what they'd say. I heard a voice call my name from behind me. I turned around to see a tall, blond Swedish god. I was hoping he was the one who'd called my name, not the little old Chinese man sitting at the table behind me. He'd been leering at me since I'd walked in, nodding at me, sending me drinks, mai tais.

"Alexandra," Thor—er, Erik—said, confirming it was him.

I nodded. He walked over, then sat down in the chair across from me. The waitress brought him a whiskey and a smile of recognition. He didn't seem to notice that I was dressed more for clubbing than for mining. "I texted you earlier," he said. "Almost two hours ago."

"I lost my phone at the Happiness Club."

This time he looked at my dress and shook his

head in disapproval. Not off to a good start. "Wheels up at first light. We have to land in Pailin early. We'll pick up our jeep there and drive into the mountains." He sipped his whiskey and sat back in the chair. "Because of your high-profile friend, we have to take a lot of back roads. Are you up for this? We're not going to be stopping at any nightclubs. We're talking about the jungles in the Cardamom Mountains."

I didn't say anything. He wouldn't believe me anyway. I thought about my trip to India six months ago and felt my shoulder twinge.

He downed his second whiskey that the waitress was more than glad to bring over to him. She stood behind him, waiting for him to order another or return her smile. He did neither. "There might be a problem with the first-light wheels up," I said. "Carter's not here."

Erik stroked his blond beard and said, "All the arrangements have been made. He better be there."

"I'm heading back to the Happiness Club to get him."

"If you and your friend Carter are here for a good time and to party, that's fine; that's your business. My business is to get you in and out of Pailin safely. Minna asked me to do this as a favor for her. I'm not going to risk my life or my plane."

"Look, the Happiness Club's owner has got Carter. I'm bringing him ten thousand dollars to let him go. I don't have time to discuss this. I've got twenty minutes to make it back there before the price goes up. I'll have him out, and we'll be waiting at the front entrance in time."

Erik waved to the waitress, who smiled and brought him another whiskey. "I'm going with you."

"Not necessary," I said.

Erik gently put his hand on my face, turned it so

he could see my blood-caked hair. "I think it's necessary if I want to get paid; we have to get Mr. Carter to the plane on time."

We paid our bill and headed back down the street. Erik didn't say a word as we walked. He pulled out a cigar. I took a deep whiff. It was Cuban. We reached the front door. It was almost three a.m. The bouncer looked me over and waved me in. As Erik followed me, the bouncer stuck his hand out to stop him. Erik grabbed his wrist, twisted it, the bouncer fell to his knees. "Okay for me to go in now?" Erik asked.

The bouncer nodded his head. Erik followed me in. The same bass-thumping song was playing. My head throbbed even more. We went up the stairs into the back room office. I knocked on the door, then heard someone say, "Enter." We opened the door to see the little man sitting behind his desk. Behind him were two men standing silently in the shadows. When the little man saw Erik, he said, "Who is this big man? Why is he here?" He reached into his desk drawer and pulled out a revolver.

I jumped in front of Erik and held the cash up. "I've got your money."

He put the revolver on his desk, pointing it out toward us. I placed the money on the desk. He smiled and thumbed through it quickly. "You know, Ms. Kustodia, it's a minute past three. I think that means you owe me another ten thousand dollars."

I glanced at the two men standing behind him. They both held their hands inside their jacket pockets. The little man reached for the revolver. I grabbed it off the desk. With my left hand, I pulled my knife out of my garter and threw it into the shoulder of his bodyguard and pointed the gun at the other bodyguard who stopped reaching for his gun and put his hands up. "I've given you what you asked for.

Where's Carter?"

The little man laughed and waved to both his bodyguards to leave the room. "I like you, Ms. Kustodia. I like you very much. Come with me. We've taken very good care of your friend."

We walked down the dark corridor lined with closed doors. From behind each door we heard moaning. We got to the last door. The little man opened it. I was hoping I wouldn't see Carter in the middle of enjoying some of the Thai nightlife. Instead, I saw Carter rolling dice on a craps table. Several Chinese businessmen and Thai prostitutes cheered him on. He rolled the dice, hitting seven and fist pumping the air. His entourage cheered as he downed another bottle of champagne. I grabbed him.

"Is the room spinning?" Carter asked, scooping up the money from the table as I pulled him toward the door. The action hero gave one last wave to his audience and leaned on my bad shoulder. I half carried him out of the club.

"One hour. The plane will be ready in an hour," Erik said, heading in the other direction.

We got back to the hotel, Carter's arm around my shoulder. He was a lot lighter than I'd imagined. He pushed me off, ran over to the curb, knelt down, and threw up. He tried to stand, knelt back down, and threw up again. I waited until the action hero was through and dragged him across the street. As we rode up the elevator together, he didn't say a word— his eyes half-shut. Then he turned and looked me over. "You clean up pretty good, Alex. I like your dress." He ran his hand along the edge of the neckline of my dress. "It's silk. It's nice."

I grabbed his wrist right before he reached my breasts. "You've had enough action for tonight, action hero."

He smiled his twenty-million-dollar smile with chunks of shrimp still in his teeth. I dragged him off the elevator and to his room. "You're welcome to spend the night," he said. "I've got a big bed. Look!" He flashed his arm around the room. He passed out and fell to the floor before I could say anything. I grabbed the blanket off the bed, threw it over him, and left the room.

Chapter Seven

Four forty-five a.m. I pounded on Tomkat's door. His bodyguard opened the door, not even checking to see who it was. He lay back down on the couch. Carter was still on the floor where I'd left him. I nudged him nicely at first and then harder. He grunted. Then I kicked him in the shin with my heavy Timberland.

"What the hell?" He sat up, clutching his shin with one hand and grabbing his head with the other.

"Time to go."

"What is it? Where are we? What time is it?"

"Look, you don't have to do this. You came. You had a good time. We all had a good time. I can catch a commercial flight back. There's no reason for you to go to Cambodia."

"Give me a minute." He rubbed his head again. "Get me a coffee."

"Get your own damn coffee. I'll meet you downstairs." I walked out, slamming the door behind me. I grabbed my backpack, checked out, and waited out in front for Erik. He showed up not more than ten minutes later. He didn't bother getting out of the Jeep. He lowered the passenger window.

"Where are your friends?" he asked with a sarcastic tone.

I stuck my head in the passenger side window. "They're on their way down."

Erik looked at me. At least the cheap evening gown was gone. I felt more comfortable in my fatigues, long-sleeve T-shirt, and hiking boots. Carter and his security stumbled out the front door. He was wearing a safari vest, short-sleeve T-shirt, cargo shorts, and Nikes. Behind him was his film crew.

As he stepped out into the front, he turned to face the cameraman. "Rough night in Thailand. We're heading out to the airstrip to get on the bush plane. From there we fly under the radar into Pailin. From this point on, I'll be filming the rest of the story on my own. It's too dangerous to bring the doc crew with." He circled his finger in the air to wrap it up. The crew handed him a briefcase and placed a wireless microphone on his T-shirt.

"Tell him we gotta go," Erik said.

I turned to Carter and said, "You might want to rethink the short sleeves and shorts. There's a big mosquito problem in Cambodia, especially where we're going. We'll be by a lot of water. You also might want to rethink the Nikes. There are a lot of snakes."

He sipped his Starbuck's that his assistant had run over to him. She also handed him a bottle of Tylenol. He chugged a couple of tablets. "I'll be fine. I've been in worse places."

I threw my backpack into the Jeep and jumped inside. Tom and his bodyguard jumped in back. A half hour later, we were climbing into Erik's twin engine Cessna. He fired up the engines. I put on my headphones. He clicked his on. "We're going to fly outside of Pailin. There's a small private strip outside the city. The casinos use it for VIPs. We should touch ground in a couple of hours."

I nodded in agreement. Tom was sound asleep. Listening to the hum of the engines, I was starting to do the same. I'd had a pretty rough night, and we were in for a long hike into the mountains. I dreamed about India and the mine. I dreamed about my great-grandfather at the imperial court. I pictured a young dark-haired woman wearing a beautiful alexandrite necklace in the arms of her lover in the moonlight as the stones turned from emerald to red. The whispered words of love turned into screams. I was jarred awake as the plane dropped. Carter was screaming. Erik was calm, flipping switches and checking dials.

He talked into the headset. "We hit an air pocket. We're near the mountains. It happens."

I watched him as he brought the plane under control. I could see he didn't spook easily. His voice was soft, almost melodic; it had a steady confidence that made me trust him. He didn't say a lot of words, but he got his point across.

We landed on the strip a short while later. There were no problems except for Carter and the airsickness bags he'd filled up. It was a cool seventy-five degrees with 99 percent humidity. As we stepped off the plane, my T-shirt clung to my skin. It was cool, but the humidity was punishing. Erik had his Range Rover waiting near the strip, loaded with our gear, water purification tablets, tents, bed nets. We were set for a couple of days up in the mountains. That's all we would need to find the best stones. I hoped.

Carter was immediately sidetracked by the flashing lights from the adjacent casinos. Before he could speak, I turned my head. "We don't have time. This is a new find. The word about the sunset rubies will get out quickly. If we're not the first to get to the mines, somebody else will buy all the best stones."

With one last look at the casino, Carter followed me over to the Range Rover, not saying a word. As we jostled around in the Rover, the terrain turned from paved city streets to jungle dirt roads. Two hours in, we reached the first village. Not much more than bamboo and straw shacks on pillars off the ground. Children played in the dirt street. They stopped and stared as the vehicle drove into the center of the village.

A crowd of dirty, unkempt children gathered around the Range Rover, sticking their hands in the window, speaking in Kola. Some of the younger men, two carrying rifles, walked up to the truck. I turned to Carter in the back seat. "Don't pull any money out. Don't talk."

I jumped out of the passenger seat. Erik got out and stood behind me; his presence was ominous. He was nearly a foot taller than the tallest of the Cambodians. Erik spoke in Kola to the older of the two young men who motioned for us to follow him to one of the largest buildings.

"Let me speak. I know what we're looking for," I told him.

Erik nodded.

We climbed up the ladder onto the bamboo deck. Grass covered the sides and the roof. An older man sat cross-legged on a mat. He nodded and greeted us in Kola, then invited us to sit down.

We sank down onto a mat across from him. "Are you hungry?" he asked.

Erik and I both replied, "Yes." This was a courtesy we had to meet before conducting any business. We ate spicy rice noodles in broth with some kind of meat I couldn't discern. After eating in silence, I finally said, "I've heard that there's a new vein of sunset rubies in this area. Do you have any we can look at?"

He called over to a woman—I assumed his wife—who was sitting in the corner. She brought over a small cloth bag. He emptied the bag onto the mat in front of us, displaying a couple hundred stones in various sizes.

"May I take a look?" I asked, pulling my loupe out of my pocket. I grabbed my pen flashlight. I knew immediately that some were composite, a mixture of glass and real corundum. Others were very low grade, a combination of rubies and sapphires. The man sitting across from me was trying to cheat me and trying to gauge if I knew it or not. While I was checking the stones out, Erik glanced over his shoulder repeatedly at the Range Rover. I checked to see what he was looking at. The two men we'd seen earlier had returned, this time with more men also carrying rifles. Erik gave me a pointed look and made a hand motion to speed things up.

In the corner, I noticed an AK-47, the weapon of choice of the Khmer Rouge. "Thank you for showing me the stones. They're not quite what we're looking for. We appreciate your hospitality and the meal." Not wanting to upset him, I added, "The man I'm working for might be interested in some of these stones. I'll have to relay to him what I've seen." I did not bother waiting for a reply. I stood up, Erik guiding me back down the ladder. As we reached the Range Rover, we saw that a crowd of children— many missing a leg or arm—were crowded around Carter who was taking selfies with them. Carter pulled his GoPro camera out of the anvil briefcase.

I grabbed the camera from his hand. "I told you to wait in the Rover."

"What's with all the cripples?" he asked, grabbing his camera back.

"We're in the middle of Khmer Rouge country. There are over six million unexploded land mines. The Khmer Rouge funded their war with gems from this area, so it's heavily mined. That's one reason I told you to wait in the car. The second is now they know you're here. They know you have money. We're leaving." I pushed him back into the car. I felt the hands crowding me, reaching forward, holding stones. Without looking at them closely, I could see that many were poor quality. I shook my head repeatedly. I felt a tug on my pant leg and saw a small boy gazing up at me. He balanced on a crude wooden crutch, his right foot missing. Unfortunately, this wasn't the first time I'd seen this kind of tragedy. It was a common scenario for the impoverished people who lived in the countries I traveled to in my search for gems. Something about this boy struck me. I think it was his bright smile, his clear eyes. He didn't look like someone who didn't know where his next meal was coming from. He slowly opened his hand, and that's when I saw the first perfect sunset ruby. I took it from him and shone my light through it. It was beautiful. I knelt down and spoke to him in Kola. "Where did you get this?"

I was surprised when he replied in English, "I can take you. I can take you."

"Where's your father? Where's your mother?"

He shook his head *no*. I opened the door and helped him into the Rover. We jumped in. Erik drove off, the boy sitting between us. Carter and Jake took the back seat. I studied the stone in my hand, admiring its color, its orange-red hue. "This is a really good stone. Are there more?" I asked him.

"Yes, there's a stream up in the mountains. I go there once a week. It takes me several days to get there," the boy replied.

"How'd you find this?" I asked.

"I was looking for food. There's a garbage dump by one of the mines. They throw out a lot of good food. I walked along the stream, two or three miles, and saw this stone. We can go, but you have to avoid the mine. The men there are very dangerous. The mine is up in the mountains where the stream starts. How much you give me?"

I figured the stone could be cut into two carats, depending on the quality and how well my grandfather could heat-treat it. It could be worth twenty to thirty thousand dollars. "Help me find more stones, and I'll make sure you get paid."

He nodded. I saw him notice my backpack on the floor and the power bars sticking out. I picked up the pack and opened the flap. "You want one?" I pulled out the power bars and handed him one.

His eyes lit up. He ripped it open and devoured it in seconds. I handed him a bottle of water. Then I reached back into my pack and handed him four more bars. He shoved them in the pocket of his ripped-up jean shorts.

The sun was starting to set. Tom Carter was snoring loudly in the back. "How much farther?" Then I realized I'd never asked the boy his name. "What's your name?"

"Kiri. My name is Kiri."

"Kiri; that means mountain peak."

He shrugged.

"How did you learn English, Kiri?"

"My parents were killed when I was little. I grew up in the orphanage run by missionaries near Pailin."

"Why did you leave?"

"The men who run the mine took me and some of the other boys to clear land mines around the mountains. I'm the last one."

I didn't know how to respond to that. His foot was healed over. He must have been very young when he stepped on the land mine. "How much farther?"

He climbed over my lap and looked out the

window. He pointed up to the base of the Cardamom Mountains. The Range Rover stopped. Erik glanced over. "This is as far as we can drive. We'll have to hike the rest of the way. We'll camp here tonight and start in the morning."

Erik set up the tents. Carter grabbed a lantern, turned it on. I grabbed it from him and turned it off. "I don't know this area. I think it's better if we stay unseen." We ate our MREs—meals ready to eat. Carter choked his down. I don't think it was up to his usual standards. Erik and Kiri didn't mind at all.

I looked over at Jake, who hadn't spoken all day. "Did you get enough to eat?"

He glanced at me and nodded his head.

"We'll leave at first light. Everybody get some sleep. Kiri, you can stay in my tent." Erik stood up and stretched.

I handed Carter and Jake mosquito nets. "Zip up your tent and use the mosquito nets."

I lay in my own tent, wrapped up in the white mosquito netting, listening to the buzzing of all the night bugs inside and outside my tent. We must be close to water. I rolled the ruby between my fingers, feeling its edges, thinking about how to cut it and what it would look like after it was treated, what piece of jewelry my father could make from it. Most women my age would hate lying on the ground in the middle of a jungle surrounded by bugs, large cats who wanted to kill me, men who would kill me for the stone I had in my hand. But this is what I lived for. The rush of finding a perfect stone.

"Get off me!" I heard the screams from the tent next to me and rushed out. I opened up the flap to see Carter swatting mosquitoes and a little three-inch snakelike lizard sitting on his chest. His arms were flailing as he looked up at me with terror in his eyes.

"Is it poisonous? Get it off me."

I reached down and picked up the tiny lizard. I brought him outside the tent and then returned to Carter who was only wearing his black compression shorts. "Where's your mosquito netting?"

He looked up at me, scratching both his arms. "I got hot."

I threw a can of bug spray at him. "This will help a little bit." I reached in my pocket and pulled out cloves of garlic. "Eat these too."

He took a whiff. "Garlic."

"You eat enough, you'll sweat it out of your skin, and it will keep about every bug away."

He shook his head.

"The sun will be rising in about another fifteen minutes. We might as well get going." As I left the tent, Erik was already striking the rest of the tents. Kiri helped. I was amazed to see how agile he was on one leg, balancing on the crutch. Years of survival, he'd learned to make do with what he had. We packed what we needed in backpacks and headed into the jungle. Erik led the way, bearing a large stick that he used to push through the tall grass to scare snakes and check for land mines. Kiri had no problem walking through the tall grass. He wasn't afraid of snakes or land mines. He probably had already seen the worst of both. He tugged on Erik's shirt and said something to him I couldn't make out. Erik looked back and motioned for us to follow. Kiri took the lead down a worn path. The sun was rising but the canopy of rubber trees sheltered us. The humidity became worse as we went deeper into the evergreen forest. My clothes clung to me, and sweat dripped off my forehead. I wiped it away before the salt could reach my parched lips.

I stopped and took a drink from my canteen. I

checked behind me. Jake was drinking out of his canteen, but I couldn't see Carter. "Jake, where's Carter?"

Jake stopped drinking and nodded off into the woods. "He went to take a leak."

Kiri hopped over and tugged on my shirt. "Miss Lady, Miss Lady."

"Kiri, call me Alex. My name is Alex."

"Miss Alex, where's your friend?"

"He had to go relieve himself. He's over there behind the evergreen."

"No! No, he can't go there!" Kiri got excited and hopped off into the woods in the direction I'd pointed.

I followed after him. Not more than fifty yards away, we saw Carter in the middle of a small open field, facing away from us, taking care of his business. "Kiri, what's wrong?"

Kiri looked around the tall grass. He walked over to a bush, picked something up, and came back to me. He was carrying a small tin sign marked with a red skull and crossbones. Written on it in Thai, French, and English: Danger, land mines.

"The path has been cleared but not off the path," Kiri said. "All these fields have land mines. You have to tell your friend to follow his footsteps back to us exactly."

I yelled to Carter, who turned around while he was in midstream. He waved over to me and smiled. "Carter, don't move!" I yelled. He zipped up, started walking toward me.

"What'd you say?"

"Stop, you idiot!" I said, "Stop!"

He stopped and stared at me with a confused look on his face. I held up the sign. I could see him mouthing the words as he read. He finally got to the

English version and then knelt over like he was trying to catch his breath. "What the hell? I didn't see that sign. What do I do?"

Jake and Erik came up behind us. "What's going on?" Jake asked.

Kiri showed him the sign. Erik took it from him and read it. "Follow your footsteps exactly to us," Erik said.

Carter looked around the four-foot-high grass. He wasn't more than a foot and a couple inches taller than it. He started to walk slowly checking the ground, looking for where he'd trampled the grass. No more than ten steps, he stopped. "I think I feel something. I heard a click." He paused. "I did. I know I heard a click."

Before I could answer him, Kiri scurried into the grass and disappeared. All we could see was the tops of the grass waving as he weaved his way through it. And, then in seconds, he was standing next to Carter. We could hear Carter. "Hey, kid, how's it going? You know a lot about mine fields, huh? You want to take a look at my right foot and see what I'm standing on?"

Kiri bent down. When he stood up, he held up a crumpled pop can. Then we heard him say, "Mr. Carter, just follow me back. Walk exactly behind me. You'll be okay."

We could see Kiri start to walk back, but Carter didn't move. His response was loud and clear, "I'm fine. I think I'll just stay here."

Kiri came back and stood in front of us. "Miss Alex, Mr. Carter won't follow me."

Erik took off, following the path Kiri had pushed down with his crutch. When he reached Carter, we saw him pick him up and throw him over his shoulder. He walked the fifty yards back to where we were standing. He placed him upright on the ground. Carter's legs wobbled and gave out. He leaned against Jake who handed him his canteen of water.

"From this point on, don't leave the path," Erik said. "If you have to take a piss, do it on the path."

Carter gulped the water and nodded his head in agreement.

We continued on our trek. Once again, Erik leading the way. By midday, we stopped. Carter was lagging behind, scratching his arms. "Are you okay?" I asked. I could see nine, ten, eleven mosquito bites, turning red, breaking through his skin. He was starting to look ill. His face was flushed, and he was sweating profusely. There was nothing I could do for him. We reached the clearing and a small stream. Kiri grabbed Erik's shirt and stopped him before he entered the clearing. I walked up to the two of them so I could hear Kiri. He pointed to a sign lying in the tall grass. Skull and crossbones just like the one we'd seen before reading Danger, Mines.

"I cleared this field. I know a safe way to walk. Follow me." Kiri took the lead at a dangerous pace, a surprising pace for a boy hopping on one leg. Not more than a couple hundred yards and we reached the stream. Carter was breathing down my back; I could hear him scratching and moaning. I wondered if he was starting to rethink his idea to join me on this journey. I took out my sluice pan, bent down in the stream, and filled it with gravel. The stream was no more than six feet across and maybe a foot deep. I swirled the water around, looking for any sign of any stones. After a couple of minutes, I could see some tiny amethyst and topaz. I sifted through the stream for hours but found nothing worth keeping. Erik watched from the sidelines, not saying anything, checking for any movement. Carter scratched and swore.

"Kiri, are you sure this is where you found the ruby?"

"Yes, it was sitting right on the side of the river bank."

"So it wasn't in the water?"

"It was on the bank."

"It probably floated down from the main mine. Can you take me to the mine?" I trudged out of the water and sat on a rock.

Kiri's face turned solemn. "Bad men there."

"Kiri, you don't have to come with me. Just tell me how to get there." When he just stared into my eyes, I continued. "I'll give you your stone back. I promise I'll pay you for it, but I need to find more like these. Like this ruby." I pulled it out of my pocket.

"The owner of the mine has a huge bagful of those. I know what they are. They are much bigger than mine," he said.

"Would he sell them to me?"

"He will sell them to whoever has the most money, but I wouldn't trust him. He might take your money and then—" Kiri stopped and looked down at his shoeless foot.

"Then what, Kiri?"

"Those men aren't to be trusted. I've seen how they treat other gem buyers."

"What other gem buyers?"

"Men from Thailand. I showed them another stone I had. I brought them to the mines because they wanted to buy more stones. They never paid me. The owner of the mine, Mr. Soko, he didn't like the price they were offering. He said the Thai men were trying to cheat him. They beat the three men and took their money. I never saw them again. I never got paid."

Erik stood silent, listening. "Alex, I didn't sign on for this. Minna asked me to get you into Cambodia, into the mines. If you still want to meet with the mine owner, that's your call, but I don't think it's a good idea. This area is full of Khmer Rouge soldiers, thieves, and murderers. The mine owners pay them to guard the mines and pay them protection money."

"The reward is worth the risk." I opened my backpack. "I've got two hundred thousand cash, and I can get more wired in if necessary. If this mine is as lucrative as Kiri is saying, they'll want to build a relationship. It's fast, easy money as long as the stones are this quality. It's worth the risk." I turned to Jake and Carter who were listening. "It's your call, Carter. It's your dime. Is your girlfriend worth this?"

Carter collapsed to the ground, moaning. I put my hand on his forehead. He was burning up. "You've got a fever, some kind of infection."

Erik grabbed Carter's arm, staring at the blistering mosquito bites. He held his hand to his forehead. "He's warm. He's got dengue fever from the mosquito bites. We have to keep him hydrated." Erik handed Carter a canteen. "He needs medical attention. He's going to get worse."

"We're a half hour from the mine, and we're six hours from the car. If word is already out about the rubies, and if they're as good as Kiri is saying, by the time I get Carter back to Pailin, they'll be sold." I watched Carter moan and roll around on the ground, then vomit, a runny mixture of mucus. "Take him back to the car. I'm going to the mine. I'll meet you back where we camped. I'll be there by tomorrow afternoon," I said.

Erik paused. "You can't go to the mine yourself. I promised Minna I'd protect you." He set up a tent and purified the stream water with tablets. He left two canteens by Carter's side and handed him a bottle of Tylenol. He looked at Jake. "Keep him hydrated. Keep him pumping water. He'll be fine." Erik handed him more water purification tablets. "Stay in the shade. Place one of these in the canteen and wait for fifteen minutes before you drink it. We'll be back in a couple of hours."

"Don't leave me. I'm dying." Carter said, grabbing Erik by the shirt.

"You're not dying. It's not fatal. It's like having a bad flu. You'll be fine." Erik stood back up.

Kiri led the way, Erik and I following behind him upstream as Carter's whimpering faded behind us. As we reached the base of the Cardamom Mountains, there were hundreds of fruit trees. This was a good sign that the mine was close. As mines are depleted, the locals plant cash crops like fruit trees. We stopped on the outskirts behind a tall tree, looking at the mine site. A large waterfall fed the stream. Underneath the waterfall there were several men panning and digging. Sitting in a small shaded hut was the man I knew I'd have to speak with. The only one not doing physical labor. Three other men walked the perimeter holding AK-47s.

Before we could decide how to proceed, Kiri stepped out from behind the tree into the compound. One of the guards pointed his gun. He recognized Kiri and put the gun down. He walked over and grabbed him by his shirt, half dragging him over to Mr. Soko. We watched at first as Mr. Soko stared at Kiri and then slapped him across the face. "Son of a bitch," I said through my teeth, reaching into my boot for my blade.

Erik touched my shoulder lightly. "No," he whispered.

Then Kiri reached in his pocket and handed Mr.

Soko the hundred-dollar bill I'd given him. Mr. Soko held it up to the light, and then Kiri pointed to where we were hiding. Mr. Soko stood up and came toward us, waving over the armed guards. Erik and I stepped out into the open with our hands up. I spoke in Kola. He answered me in English. "You have money."

I opened my backpack and showed him the stacks of hundred-dollar bills, still in their bands. This was the moment. Either we'd strike a relationship or he'd take the money and the three of us would be dead. Before he could make that decision, I said, "I want to buy everything you have, and I want to buy everything you will find. This is just the start. I have many buyers." We were still breathing, so I think Mr. Soko decided a long-term relationship would be beneficial.

He smiled and led us back to his tiny straw hut. A small woman quickly brought us tea, bowing and nodding. She set it on the low table in front of us and scurried away. I pulled out the ruby that Kiri had given me. "I am looking for more stones like this one."

"Where'd you get this?" Mr. Soko asked.

When I didn't answer, he looked over at Kiri. He looked like he was going to hit Kiri again. "I bought it from a dealer in Pailin," Erik said. "General Hun Sun referred me to him."

"You know the general?" Mr. Soko asked.

"I've had dealings with him," Erik said.

The little woman scurried back over, carrying a cloth bag that she handed to Mr. Soko. He emptied the stones on the small wood table in front of him. Thousands of carats of deep orange-red sunset rubies lay before me. I motioned to the stones. "May I take a closer look?"

He nodded. The first five stones I examined with

my loupe and light were magnificent. Some of the larger ones weren't as fine, but the smaller ones, two even three carats, were worth tens of thousands of dollars. I did a quick calculation in my head, wanting to start low enough to get a good price but not too low as to insult him. I made a pile of at least a hundred stones. "How much?" I asked.

He rifled through the stones like they were an abacus, touching the edges, figuring their worth in carats and in money. He took out a small calculator, typed in a number and turned it so I could read it. Four hundred thousand.

"Too much," I said, shaking my head.

He handed me the calculator. I typed in one hundred fifty thousand and turned it around. He shook his head. It was a fair price for both of us. Fair enough I could tell he wasn't angry but excited. Taking the calculator, he typed in a number and handed it back to me. Two hundred fifty thousand.

I put the calculator down. "These hundred stones? You can find more of this quality?" I asked.

He pointed around him to the miners who were sifting through the sand, gravel, and dirt. "I can find all the stones you want," he said.

"I'll give you my final price. You can keep those other stones. I want to bring back these hundred to show my boss. He'll be happy with these, and he will want to work with you. My final price is two hundred thousand."

He thought, sipped his tea, and agreed with a big smile. I stacked the cash in front of him and grabbed the stones as he was counting.

Erik whispered, "Let's move."

By the time Mr. Soko was finished counting, Erik, Kiri and I were back under the cover of the forest, moving quickly. In a half hour's time, we met up with Carter and Jake. "Don't bother packing. Just go," Erik said.

"Mr. Carter's pretty sick," Jake said.

Erik pulled Carter off the ground by his collar. Holding him half up as he walked at a fast pace, we headed back. After five hours walking at a steady pace, we made it to the Range Rover. The hood was open. Erik ran to look at it. "Damn!"

I ran up and stared under the hood. I could see it had been cleaned out; the battery, belts and hoses were missing. The back window was smashed. The rest of our supplies were gone.

Erik leaned against the Rover. He glanced up at the sky. "We got an hour of light left. I've got a couple of tarps. We can make tents for tonight. We'll have to keep a fire going so the smoke will keep away the mosquitoes."

Carter, Kiri and Jake lay down in the back of the Range Rover. I sat on the ground near Erik. We polished off the power bars from my backpack. Erik made a fire. We hung a tarp from the top of the Range Rover and used a couple of large branches to make a canopy. Erik and I sat on the ground in front of the fire. "You think it's safe to have the fire?"

"Everyone knows we're here by now," Erik said. "I'm more concerned about keeping the cats and the mosquitoes away." He went off into the woods and came back carrying an armful of clumpy dirt. He threw it on the fire.

"What's that?" I asked.

"It's termite mounds. The smell from the burning mounds keeps the mosquitoes away."

I could understand why. It smelled like raw sewage burning. I could hear Carter gagging and throwing up inside the Range Rover. The termite mounds worked. I didn't hear or feel any mosquitoes or flies around me. I was exhausted, but I couldn't sleep. I watched as Erik stoked the fire. He was humming something I couldn't make out. "What are you singing?" I asked.

"It's an old Swedish song. My mom used to sing it to me. In English, it translates something like the birds have eaten all the lingonberries, so how will we make our pie?"

I couldn't help but laugh. He smiled as he crouched down in front of the fire, poking at it with a stick. He came back and sat down next to me, leaning his back against the Range Rover. He took his cigar out of his pocket, bit the tip, lit it and took a puff. "Cuban?" I asked.

He nodded with the cigar in his mouth, puffing away.

"Do you have another one?" I asked.

He looked surprised, reached in his shirt pocket, and handed me another.

I bit off the tip as he handed me his cigar to light mine. I leaned back, puffing. "Very nice. Thank you. This isn't quite the trip I was expecting," I said.

"How'd you get involved with this asshole?" Erik asked, nodding his head toward the Rover where Carter was.

"My family has a jewelry store in Chicago. That's where I'm from. He contacted my father to make a custom necklace for his girlfriend. He insisted on coming with us and filming the trip." I breathed in as Erik took a puff of his cigar, then asked, "How do you know Minna?"

"I've known her for years. We've worked together. I've been her pilot and guide on a lot of gem-hunting expeditions."

We sat for a while enjoying our cigars. "This is good, but I could use a glass of Stoli to go with it."

"If you make it Absolut, I'll join you," he said. "Why don't you sleep? I'll keep watch." He reached into his jacket pocket, pulled out a .45, loaded the chamber, and set it on his lap.

"Okay," I said. "Why don't you wake me in a couple of hours?"

He never did. I woke up the next morning to the sound of Erik striking camp. Carter looked worse than the night before. Kiri walked out of the woods, his arms full of longan fruit.

"Dragon's eye," Kiri said, placing them at my feet. He took one, peeled the skin, and ate the sweet jelly of the fruit. Erik and I followed his example. It was refreshing.

"What do we do now?" I asked Erik.

"We start walking back to Pailin."

Kiri interrupted. "There's a bus that stops by the big waterfall once a day. It's not more than three or four hours' walk from here." Kiri pointed down the road where it split. We followed his lead. By afternoon, we were in front of the Elephant Head Waterfall. There was a bench with a bus stop. Several Chinese tourists were taking pictures of the waterfall. Their cameras turned to us when they saw Tom Carter, who perked up.

"Quick, kid, get my GoPro from my backpack," Carter said. Kiri hopped over and pulled the camera out of the backpack. Carter showed him how to use it. "Hit this button and aim it at me," Carter said. Then he turned and spoke into the camera. "We made it out of the mines. The heavily armed men tracked us into the forest, but we were able to outmaneuver them. As you can see, I'm pretty beat up, sustained some injuries, but overall I'm okay."

Erik and I exchanged looks. I could see Erik mouthing the word "asshole" as Carter continued, signing autographs and posing for pictures with the tourists.

When the bus arrived, it was crowded, but we made room. I gave up my seat so Carter could sit. I clung to the ceiling strap while Erik stood behind me. We bumped into each other as the bus jostled along the uneven dirt roads. He put his arm around me to steady me and pressed up against my back. I could smell cigar and musk. Both smells were pleasant and intoxicating, and I breathed him in as I watched out the window. I saw several armed Cambodian soldiers walking along the roadway.

"Did I do good, Miss Alex?" Kiri asked, standing next to me.

I bent down. "Kiri, you did very good." I adjusted the weight of my backpack on my shoulder. Inside was at least five hundred thousand dollars worth of sunset rubies.

A few hours later, we stood at the airstrip outside Pailin as Erik arranged to refuel the plane. A doctor from the casino came out to the strip and examined Carter in the small office. I sat with Kiri outside on the wood bench.

He smiled a bright smile. His dirty little face was handsome, even with his shaggy black hair covering his face. I pushed the hair away, revealing his clear black eyes. "The stone you found is worth a lot of money. What are you going to do with it?" I asked him.

"I can find a room and get some food and maybe I can go to the school in Pailin."

"Why do you want to go to school?"

"I want to be a doctor. There's a lot of children like me who need help."

"Wait here," I said. I went over to Erik, who was completing his preflight check of the plane.

"You did okay at the mine. When I first met you, I thought you were going to be trouble, but you did okay." His broken English Swedish accent was endearing. He gave me a crooked half smile that made him more attractive.

"Do you have room on the plane for one more?"

He looked over to the office where Kiri was staring at us. "What are you going to do with him?"

"I have a friend in the states, who's a surgeon at Chicago's Rehab Institute. He does a lot of pro bono work, fitting kids with prosthetics. I want him to meet Kiri, and I want Kiri to tell him about the rest of his village."

Erik's smile grew bigger. "Yeah, you are okay."

For the first time in a long time, I felt an urge I couldn't hold back. I kissed him. More as a thank-you, but if I was being honest with myself, I wanted to kiss him the minute he'd walked into the Bamboo Room. I wanted to feel his heart beating next to mine again. The first kiss was my idea, the second, third and fourth were his.

Chapter Eight

Kiri grabbed my arm tightly as the plane made its descent into Midway Airport. He'd spent the whole flight looking out windows and pacing up and down the aisle. His view of the world before was the five-mile radius surrounding his village. He'd only seen the lights of the big city of Pailin. I had contacted my friend, Michael Angellico, and scheduled a consultation to examine Kiri to fit him with a prosthetic foot. Kiri was very excited. He asked if he could have a special foot made for playing soccer.

When the door opened, the documentary crew got off first. I could see them set up their equipment facing the open plane door. A crowd of photographers gathered behind them. Carter grabbed Kiri's hand and led him off the plane. I watched as he waved to the crowd while cameras went off. Kiri turned around to look at me. I was standing in the doorway waiting to exit. I could hear Carter whisper, "Okay, Kenny, smile for the cameras, okay?"

I nodded to Kiri. Carter positioned himself in front of the documentary crew. When his assistant clipped a microphone to his collar, Carter rolled his finger in the air, signaling to start filming. "We've landed back in Chicago. Not only did we find the stones we were looking for, but we rescued this young boy."

He hesitated, and I said from behind him, "Kiri."

Kiri waved to the people who snapped more photos. Carter continued, "I went to Cambodia for an adventure to hunt for gems in the jungles of the

Cardamom Mountains, and what I found was hundreds of children just like Kiri forced to clear land mines—some of them like Kiri missing limbs, going hungry every night. That's something I couldn't walk away from. They can't walk, and I can't walk away from them."

Behind him, I took a deep breath.

"That's why I'm launching a foundation to help the lost children of Cambodia to give them a hand, to give Kiri a foot. It's called *Give a Hand, Give a Foot.* This documentary will be part of the fund-raising campaign. And I ask my fellow Hollywood friends to give back, to give big, to give a hand, give a foot. Thank you." He waved his finger to wrap up.

Carter let go of Kiri, left him and went to talk to some of the reporters.

"Miss Alex, what was that about?" Kiri asked me.

"Mr. Carter volunteered to pay for your new foot. We'll make sure you get a good one for playing soccer. Come on, Kiri." I led him through the gate.

I was surprised to see my father waiting for us at arrivals. He stood by baggage claim and managed a forced smile when he saw me. His eyes didn't light up like they usually do when he sees me, especially when I return from an expedition. He wrapped his large arms around me and held me in a big hug, not letting go. I kissed his cheek and pulled back. "Father, this is the boy I emailed you about, Kiri. Kiri, this is my father."

Kiri stared up like he was looking up from the bottom of a skyscraper. He held out his hand. "Nice to meet you, sir."

My father knelt down in slow motion, looked the boy in the eye, and shook his hand, which was no larger than my father's thumb. "Nice to meet you, Kiri. Alexandra emailed me all about you. You are most welcome."

"Father, I didn't expect to see you." I listened as the alarms signaling the start of the baggage carousel went off. "Grandfather was supposed to pick us up."

He took my arm and led me to the seats that lined the wall by the baggage claim. "Sit, Alexandra."

"Father, you're making me nervous. What's wrong? Is everything okay?"

"Your grandfather's dead."

"What? What happened?" I breathed in. I felt as if I'd been punched in the stomach.

"Someone broke into his house late at night, tied him up, and beat him."

"Why? Who?"

"The police think it may have been whoever broke into the store. When he couldn't get into the safe, he went to grandfather's house to get the combination, and your grandfather wouldn't give it up."

I turned my head so my father couldn't see my tears. He put his big arms around me. "Malenkaya, that's who your grandfather was. He was a very brave man."

"He wasn't brave. He was stupid. Why didn't he just give them the combination for the safe? Everything in there is replaceable." I sat silently trying to absorb the news. I wasn't prepared. He wasn't sick. He hadn't lingered in a hospital bed or in hospice. There'd been no warning. He was here, and then he was taken from us. "Why didn't you tell me?"

"I didn't want to tell you while you were flying. I wanted to tell you in person. Minna was the one who called to let me know."

"Minna found grandfather?"

"She'd been calling him all morning and got worried when he didn't answer. She went to check on him and found Hunter in the backyard, growling and barking. Then she found your grandfather."

We grabbed my bags and went to my father's car. We headed onto Stevenson Expressway toward downtown Chicago. Kiri stared out the window. When we reached the city, his eyes were wide open, looking at the buildings and the people.

"Are you hungry?" I asked him.

He nodded.

We drove through Al's Beef. Kiri could not conceive of the fact that you could drive up to a window with your car and get food. It was beyond his capacity to understand such abundance, such decadence. He polished off his Italian beef and his Coke. I had no appetite. When we arrived at the store, my father unlocked the door and let us in. Kiri walked around to all the glass display cases, inspecting the stones.

"I found one of these. That's a sapphire; that's a citrine." He pointed out all the stones he'd found around his village.

"You have a very good eye if you can recognize these gems when they're in their natural state. Most people would step right over them, thinking they were just pebbles," my father said.

"Do you fix the stones here? I've never seen anyone with the gems finished like this. They're usually dirty and dull. How do you make them shiny like this? How do you cut them like this?" Kiri asked, firing off questions.

"I can show you how we cut and polish the stones and how we make this beautiful jewelry," my father said.

"My father is an expert jeweler," I said. "If you like, maybe he can take you in the back room and show you the tools he uses to make the jewelry."

"Yes, I would like that," Kiri said.

After my father showed Kiri the equipment, we went up to his apartment over the store. He made us some tea. With all the talk about my grandfather, I had forgotten to show my father the reason we'd gone to Cambodia. I retrieved the bag from my backpack and placed it on the coffee table. The sunset ruby stones spilled out, a dazzling array of color. My father pulled his chair up closer to the coffee table, took out his loupe, and examined each stone.

"Alexandra, these are beautiful. I've never seen a color like this."

"Father, can you heat-treat them? I know grandfather always did the heat-treating for rubies."

"We can do it together. I can show you what he taught me. I'm not my father, but I've done it enough times to be able to teach you. These will make a beautiful infinity necklace. Then a Kustodia piece will walk the red carpet. When they ask 'Who are you wearing?' they will answer Kustodia," my father said. "I wish your grandfather was here to see these stones. He would have been very proud of you. He was always proud of you. This necklace will be a tribute to his eternal memory."

"The rest of the stones we can buy from Carter to make into rings and earrings. He paid two hundred thousand for all the stones plus our expenses. I think once they're cut and treated, they'll easily be worth over a million dollars," my father said.

I thought about my grandfather and how much he would have loved to see these sunset rubies. I pulled up the right leg of my jeans. Around my ankle was my tattoo anklet of gems, each one representing a part of the world I'd traveled to and an adventure I'd had in that country. Each stone, like the story it told, was unique. The last one on the anklet was my alexandrite from India. Right next to it I would place this ruby. Inside the ruby, the initials "AK" for my grandfather, Alexander Kustodia, because that stone would always remind me of the day he was murdered.

Chapter Nine

We gathered at the Russian Orthodox Church on
the near north side. The church, carved from Chicago
limestone, had the recognizable onion-shaped domes
common to Russian Orthodox churches. It was the
place we celebrated weddings, christenings, and dark
days like this, funerals. The bells rang in a series
from high to low, summoning mourners and
mourning the passage of my grandfather.

As we entered the nave, we walked down the
center aisle. My grandfather lay out in the mahogany
coffin. It was an open casket. Mourners—some I
knew, some I didn't—gathered in front of the coffin.
Each one bowed and kissed the ribbon on his
forehead, an old Russian custom. Minna appeared
dressed in black and sobbing. She stood in front of
my grandfather and bent down. She spoke softly into
his ear for several minutes. I went up to her and put
my arm around her. When she turned to look at up at
me, I saw the necklace—a beautiful eternity circle of
stones, each one a perfect alexandrite. I'd never seen
her wear it before.

I couldn't take my eyes off it. The incandescent
lights of the church turned the stones from green to a
deep red. With tears in her eyes, she gazed up at me,
dotting at them with her linen monogrammed
handkerchief. She spoke in Russian. She stopped
crying, not wanting me to see her. "Your grandfather
was a very good man."

"Come; let's go. Let's have some tea and sit and

talk." I led Minna back to the sitting room where we had laid out tea and cookies. I had known her since I was a little girl. She'd been best friends with my grandmother and did business with my grandfather. More than that, she was my mentor.

"Alexandra, your trip. All went well? Erik helped you?"

"Yes, Erik was very helpful. I was able to buy many perfect sunset rubies. My father is creating a necklace for Tom Carter."

"This is good. Very good."

"What about you, Minna? My father told me you found my grandfather. That must have been quite horrible."

Minna nodded. "Yes, it was." Minna dabbed at her eyes with her handkerchief.

I couldn't stop staring at the necklace. I had to ask. "The necklace is beautiful."

She unclasped it and handed it to me. I studied it, turning it around. Its craftsmanship was a work of art. Each stone was faceted expertly so when the light struck, it reflected brilliantly. On the gold clasp was the wolf, our family crest. "This is amazing. Did my grandfather make it for you?"

"No, his father made it in in the old country. After your grandmother died, I went back with him on many buying trips. Every time we returned to Russia, he would search the pawn shops, jewelry stores, and black market looking for any of his father's pieces. All of them had been taken by the Bolsheviks. He found this necklace in a small store outside Kungur. Your grandfather had searched for it for forty years."

I held the cool stones in my hand, sifting them through my fingers like rosary beads. I can imagine my grandfather's face when he found this necklace, *the* necklace. The necklace I'd heard stories about as long as I could remember. I didn't know why he hadn't shown it to my father or me. "My grandfather's told me about this necklace my whole life. How come he never showed it to us?"

"After your grandmother died, your grandfather was very lonely. Our business relationship became more than business. You have to understand that he never stopped loving your grandmother. He never stopped mourning her, and he vowed to never remarry out of respect for her. The necklace was his way of telling me that I was special to him, that he loved me in the only way he could. He wanted to keep our relationship secret, so he didn't want to tell you about the necklace."

I went to hand the necklace back to Minna. She pushed my hand back. "Now that he's gone, the necklace belongs to you. I carry his memory, but the necklace needs a new story. You're the new story," she said. "He'd want you to have it. It's a part of your family history."

I halfheartedly tried to give it back to her again. She grabbed it and stood up. She was only five feet tall but was incredibly strong. She walked back around my chair, moved my hair off my neck onto my shoulder, placed the necklace over me, and clasped it. I could feel her strong grip on my shoulder.

"This is for you, Alexandra," Minna said, placing her fingers gently on the stones around my neck.

I put my hand over hers. "Thank you; it's beautiful."

We went back to the chapel. The pallbearers gathered around the casket. My father said a prayer before closing the casket lid. The pallbearers carried my grandfather out to the small cemetery adjacent to the churchyard. The plot next to my grandmother's site had been dug out. The smell of fresh dirt filled my nostrils. My grandfather was really gone, dead. I'd been saying *gone* all this time like he'd left on a buying trip and would walk into the store carrying a bag of diamonds, smiling and telling stories of his trip. No more stories.

After the priest said a few words and a prayer, the coffin was lowered into the ground and the mourners dropped flowers and a handful of dirt on the coffin. I watched the procession. My father sat next to me, acknowledging each one with a nod of his head. As they walked by, mourners whispered, "May his memory be eternal."

When it was our turn to say our final goodbye, my father noticed the necklace. "Alexandra, where did you get that?" he whispered, touching it.

"Minna gave it to me."

"I know that necklace." Holding hands, we walked up to the grave. My father dropped a rose, whispered a prayer, and dropped a handful of dirt as a gentle rain began. A sign that my grandfather would be joining my grandmother in heaven. Another Russian superstition I didn't believe in. A roar of thunder rang out, a sign my grandfather had made it.

Now it was my turn. I looked around the graveyard. I shivered like a goose was stepping over my grave as my grandmother used to say. I turned around to see the goose. What I saw was the shadow of a man watching from a distance on the edge of the woods adjacent to the cemetery. I stared at him for what seemed like minutes. Neither one of us breaking our gaze. The sun set behind him, the oak trees of the forest casting long shadows that crawled along the gravestones. The shadow man disappeared into the darkness.

Chapter Ten

Four weeks later, I touched down at LAX. When I got to baggage claim, I saw a limo driver holding a sign with my name spelled with a *C*. Carrying only my backpack and a million-dollar necklace, I followed the limo driver to his car. He drove me to the Four Seasons in Beverly Hills. A uniformed doorman opened the entry door and escorted me to the registration desk. The young woman behind the computer monitor smiled and greeted me.

"Your reservation is all taken care of, Ms. Kustodia," she said. "You're in the penthouse suite. Mr. Carter arranged everything personally."

Of course he did. I certainly didn't need the penthouse suite for one night but didn't want to argue. Despite my protests, the bellboy insisted on leading me to my room.

Entering the room, I noticed a basket with chocolate-covered strawberries and champagne sitting on the coffee table. I was not accustomed to this opulence nor did I need it. My father was better at dealing with the clients than I was. It had taken us four weeks—my father and I—to heat-treat the rubies. I now knew the family secret. The centuries-old Russian process brought out the brilliant orange and red color of the stones. After we were done, my father labored day and night cutting each stone to be a perfect match. Out of all the pieces my father has cut and created, this was his masterpiece. I opened its case and stared at it. Then I put it on. It seemed a shame to part with it.

I walked into the bathroom, staring at myself in the mirror. My black T-shirt and worn jeans understated the brilliance of the million-dollar necklace. Hot and tired from the flight, I ran a bath, a luxury I don't usually indulge in, but after seeing the nightly rate on the back of the door, I thought I should make the most of the room. I left the champagne bottle on the table and opened the bar fridge. I grabbed the ice-cold Ketel One vodka. I left the glass and headed to the bathroom. I undressed and sunk into the bubble bath, still wearing the necklace.

I touched the stones, and a surge of electricity ran through me. I felt faint. The room swirled around me, blending into a kaleidoscope of colors, and then everything went dark. I could hear the jungle. I could smell the Cuban cigar, the sweat, the musk. I could hear the heartbeat. It had been more than a month since I'd kissed Erik. I could still feel the pressure of his lips on mine. His chest pressed against my chest. His sky-blue eyes, the color of London blue topaz. His long blond hair brushing against his broad shoulders.

The phone rang. I opened my eyes. I reached up on the wall behind me and grabbed it. "Hello."

On the other end was the perky girl at the registration desk. "Ms. Kustodia, Mr. Carter is here to see you."

"Send him up." I jumped out of the tub and draped myself in the large bathrobe. I hurriedly dried myself off and put my clothes back on. I ran my fingers through my hair and glanced at my face in the mirror. It would have to do. I took off the necklace and put it in its case just as the knock sounded on the door.

I opened it to see the action hero looking in better shape than when I left him last. His bodyguard Jake stood guard in the hall. I waved to Jake. He gave me a smile.

"Alex, you look great. Thank you for coming out," Carter said, entering the room and sitting on the couch before I could say anything.

I brought over the necklace box and sat down next to him.

With a jittery leg, Carter reached for the box. "So, how'd it turn out? My girlfriend is really excited. She found the perfect dress to go with the necklace based on the drawings your father sent me. My publicist has already put out the story of how I found the stones and the pictures of me in the village with the children. My charity is setting up a program for the children of the village to fund a school."

"That's great." Maybe he wasn't so bad after all.

"Hey, that kid you brought home, you know, Kevin? You think I could borrow him for some photo ops?"

Then I went back to my original opinion of him. "He underwent surgery for a prosthetic foot. He's in rehab."

"That's too bad." Carter paused. Then he rubbed his hands together. "Can I see it?"

I opened the box and turned it toward him. It was just the right angle for the afternoon sun splashing through the large windows.

"Wow," he said, grabbing the case. "It was worth the trouble. These are great. Your father's an artist." He snapped the case closed. "Listen, I want you at the premiere tonight. The whole red-carpet deal. I want to introduce you. You can help sell the story."

"I didn't bring anything to wear. I thought I was just dropping off the necklace."

"Don't worry about it. I'll have my assistant bring over a couple of dresses." He gave me an appraising glance. "You're what? Thirty-eight *D*, size six?"

I had no answer for him. I was uncomfortable talking about my bra size, but surprisingly he was right. "Okay."

"Okay then." He shoved the necklace box in his leather jacket pocket and took off.

I called my dad to check on him and Kiri. Both were doing fine. After I got off the phone, I took Minna's alexandrite necklace out of my backpack and put it on. If I was going to walk the red carpet, I wanted to look the part. My father had made me a matching pair of earrings with some of the alexandrite I'd found in India.

A short while later, I was dressed in an emerald-green form-fitting dress the stylist had dropped off. I spent an hour with Carter's stylist and hair artist who talked me into piling my hair in a chignon. I usually would argue, but it left my neck bare to show off the alexandrite. I stood in front of the full-length mirror in the hallway of my room, turning and twisting, looking myself over. I looked like my mother—at least what I could remember of her when she was not much older than I am now, shortly before she died. The scar on my left shoulder was barely visible with the foundation the makeup artist had covered it with. The fresh tattoo on my ankle still burned a bit. I'd added the sunset ruby to my charm bracelet tattoo. I had started the tattoo when I'd found my first perfect sapphire in Mozambique. The tattoo was more about the adventure than the actual stone. The sapphire was interwoven with the image of a lioness I had encountered in Mozambique. It was dusk, and she was out starting her hunt. I had stayed too long at the mine by myself even though my guide had warned me of the nearby pride of lions that hunted at night. I couldn't let it go. I could never let it go. She chased me up into a tree where I spent the night as she circled below, letting out low, soft roars. I should have been terrified, but for some reason I was comforted by her sound. I fell asleep. That next morning, I started the anklet tattoo. Each stone was a visible reminder of one of my gem hunts. The sunset ruby reminded me of Kiri and Erik but most of all— my grandfather.

I walked down to the lobby. Out of the corner of my eye, I watched the men watching me. I headed out to the waiting limo that Carter had sent over. I opened the bottle of Ketel One. Carter was thorough, or maybe it was his assistant again.

There was a line of cars in front of the TCL Chinese Theaters. Spotlights shot into the evening sky. The red carpet lay under a canopy of red balloons. The sign on the marquee read, "Premiere Tonight: Tom Carter's *Blood and Glory*." Fans pushed up against the velvet rope as paparazzi shot photos. I sat in the limo, not knowing what to do. The driver got out and opened the door. Immediately a thousand cameras turned on me and clicked. I could hear some of the fans whispering, "Who's that? Is she in the movie?"

And then another limo pulled up behind me. Tom Carter jumped out of the back, and the crowd erupted into a cheer. All the photographers turned his way. He reached his hand into the limo and escorted his girlfriend onto the carpet. She was slightly taller than him even though she was wearing flats. She wore a beautiful, sequined scarlet dress. The ruby necklace flashed orange-red fire as the lights from the cameras danced on it. The necklace outshone everything around it, even Carter's star power. Carter motioned for me to come over to him as a reporter stuck a microphone in his face. He spoke into it, his words rushed.

"This is my guide. The gem hunter who helped me find the stones for this necklace. This is Alexandra Kustodia. Her father created this necklace. The only one like it in the world. Sunset rubies. The rarest rubies."

His girlfriend smiled and posed for the cameras, hand on her hip, head tossed back. I took a step back, slouched down a bit, not wanting to be taller than Carter. As the cameras clicked, I smiled. We made our way into the theater. After watching the movie, Carter invited me to the after-party. I declined. I went back to my hotel, took off my designer gown, and threw on a T-shirt. I lay on the bed, wrapping my finger around the alexandrite necklace. Then I stopped. This was the necklace my grandfather had told me about since I was a little girl. This was the necklace my great-grandfather had made for the Grand Duke who had given it to his secret love. This was the necklace that held the secret love letter. I took it off and grabbed my loupe out of my backpack. I looked on the back of the stones. Nothing was visible. According to my grandfather's story, the stones revealed the message only by candlelight.

I turned off the lights, pulled out my Bic lighter and ran it in front of the stones as I checked the back, waiting to see the last love letter of an imperial Grand Duke. There was nothing on the back of the stones except for small scratches on them just above the girdle. Normal wear for a hundred-year-old piece. I grabbed my cell phone and called Minna.

The voice on the other end sounded weary. My grandfather's death had hit her just as hard as the rest of the family. "Minna, it's Alexandra."

"Yes, my dear."

"I'm in Hollywood."

"Your father told me."

"The ruby necklace turned out beautifully. Carter announced to the cameras that it was a Kustodia piece," I told her, swirling the liquid around in the glass I held.

"That's wonderful, my girl. That's wonderful for the store."

"I wore the alexandrite necklace on the red carpet. It got almost as much attention as the ruby necklace." I paused. "Minna, were the stories my grandfather told about the alexandrite necklace just stories? Were they fairy tales for a young girl?"

"Your grandfather liked to tell stories."

"There's no love letter on the back. I don't see any secret message." I ran the necklace through my fingers.

Minna laughed for a moment. "I'm sure that at some time there might have been an inscription. Perhaps 'I love you' or a special date. That's not unusual. Your grandfather was a romantic. He might have stretched the truth a bit."

"It's a beautiful necklace. Thank you again for giving it to me." I put it back around my neck.

"I want you to make a new romantic story with the necklace. Find someone you love as much as the Grand Duke loved his beloved."

I blushed. I was a bit uncomfortable talking about romance with Minna. "Either way, it's beautiful. I cherish and love it. I'm going to do some research on the Grand Duke and the necklace so I can get a better history of it."

"That's fine, dear. I'm very tired now. Goodnight," Minna said, hanging up.

I put my phone on the nightstand, lay back, and felt the cool weight of the alexandrites in my fingers. Secret message or not, this necklace was part of my family history. I don't go in for Russian superstition or folk tales, but I could feel the energy of the necklace—its history, the people who touched it. Maybe it was my blood connection to my great-grandfather who crafted it, who hunted the stones in the darkness like I do. Something in our family DNA creates this obsession I—we—have to hunt gems, whether its tracking emeralds in Cleopatra's old mines or fishing for sapphires in a deep lake in Sri Lanka. It's not the beauty of the stones but how they are created.

I lifted my leg up in the air, admiring my anklet tattoo, pondering the journey these gems had taken me on. This emerald... one of the first stones I'd ever found. Its deep green shade is from the addition of chromium to its chemical formula, an addition made only by the unlikely meeting of two opposite plates shifting directions. Or this opal found in the outback of Australia, shining red from the spheres in its silica gel. And this sapphire dredged from the bedrock and washed down a river after millions of years. Finally, the more recent sunset ruby, glowing an orange red on my ankle. Hundreds of millions of years to create one perfect stone. Each one requiring a perfect collision of elements, time and pressure. Are these stones an accident of nature? Or a predetermined event? I drifted off.

That night, I dreamed a dream I haven't had since I was a little girl. It was the first time my grandfather told me the story of the necklace. It was the same night of my first ballet recital. I dreamed I was dancing for the imperial family at the Bolshoi. I was Clara in *The Nutcracker*. In the front row, the Romanov family sat quietly holding hands, watching every move as I danced. I could see their sad, solemn faces. Czarina Alexandra was trying to tell me something—her mouth moved, but no words came out. Each time I twirled, I strained to hear what she was saying. As I danced and spun, I became dizzy, leaping about the stage. The dream turned into a nightmare. Their faces changed into horrifying mutilations, decaying skin. The faces of corpses. In my dream, I fell, landing on my bad shoulder. I woke up in a sweat, my shoulder throbbing. I checked my phone. It was three a.m. It was the same hour I'd woken up when I was a little girl. My grandmother told me three a.m. was the devil's hour because it was exactly twenty-four hours opposite of the hour Christ died on the cross. I still didn't believe in Russian superstition, but some shadow had come over me since my grandfather had been murdered. A shadow that was haunting me. Even now I felt the shadow staring at me from the dark corners of the room, crawling up the wall like a maleficent spider. I got up, opened the curtains, and glanced out the window overlooking the street. The streetlights flickered. A storm was rolling in, unusual for drought-stricken LA. I wanted a drink to kill the pain. I hadn't taken a pain pill in months. The doctor said my shoulder would never be one hundred percent again. I could hear it catch when I raised my arm overhead.

I'd cleaned out the minibar earlier. I needed fresh air and something to drink. I pulled on my jeans and threw a T-shirt on. Walking out of the hotel, I headed down Rodeo Drive. During the day, this street was crowded, but now there was no one around, nothing was open. The stores were empty, lights dim—no sound other than my footsteps pounding on the pavement. I kept walking to get away, to clear my head, but the shadow followed me.

Chapter Eleven

I thanked the Uber driver as he pulled in front of Chicago's world famous Rehab Institute on Superior Drive. He'd picked me up from the airport and brought me straight here. I was anxious to check on Kiri, who'd been fitted with his new foot. The volunteer at the front desk directed me to the rehab area where Kiri was working with his therapist. I followed the maze of hallways down the long corridors.

When I got to the rehab room, I peeked through the window. Kiri was hanging onto a railing, stepping tentatively on his new foot. From the sidelines, my father watched nervously. I opened the door and walked into the room. Kiri and his therapist both turned to look at me. Kiri struggled to retain his balance as he tipped forward, turning toward the door. "Miss Alex!" he exclaimed, stepping off the board and balancing himself on his new carbon graphite foot.

"Hi, Kiri, I wanted to stop here first and see how you were doing before I went home." I set my backpack down on the floor beside me.

"No crutches!" He slowly walked toward me, balancing carefully, his arms extended.

"I see that. You're doing great." I marveled as he stood in front of me. I knelt down, and he wrapped his arms around my neck. I returned his hug, quickly releasing him.

"He's progressing very well. I told him he'd be

playing soccer in no time," his therapist said, smiling at both of us.

"We watched you on the red carpet last night," Kiri said. "Me and Pappa."

"Pappa?" I looked at my father.

My father shrugged. "Kiri's doing great. You wouldn't know it's his first day of therapy with his new foot."

As Kiri went back to the balancing rail, I pulled my father out into the hall. "Carter loved the necklace. I had a lot of questions from reporters about our jewelry, about the store and your work."

"That's great, Alexandra. That's really great," my father said as he looked over my shoulder into the window, keeping an eye on Kiri. "We've already had several calls today. We might need to hire some help. I haven't been able to return many of the calls. I've been working on your grandfather's estate." He reached into his coat pocket and pulled out a piece of paper. "I cleared out your grandfather's safety deposit box. I found this."

Taking the piece of paper from him, I read in English. It was a handwritten order of commission for an alexandrite infinity necklace signed by Grand Duke Ferdinand Romanov. I was not surprised to see it written in English rather than Russian. Members of the imperial court preferred French or English as they considered Russian the language of peasants. Many of them, including the czar's children, didn't even learn their native language.

"Don't you see, Alexandra? This has to be the commission paper for the necklace you're wearing. The Grand Duke was the one who commissioned the necklace. The one from your grandfather's story."

"Wait." I peered closer at the paper. "This isn't from grandfather's store. The name is different."

"Of course it is. Your great-grandfather changed the family name when he came to America."

"Why didn't I know this?" All these years, and I'd never heard about changing the family name?

"Your great-grandfather was escaping the Bolsheviks who were killing anyone even associated with the Romanovs. He had to keep our family name a secret even long after the revolution. No one spoke our original name, Volkov."

"Volkov." I thought for a moment. "That means Wolf. That's where our family crest comes from." Now I understood.

"Yes." He paused and then said, "I did some research on Ferdinand Romanov. He wasn't just a Grand Duke; he was the czar's cousin and also the keeper of the imperial purse."

"Keeper of the imperial purse?" I repeated.

"A very important job in those days. He was responsible for the czar's finances, including the czarina's jewels and treasures," my father explained.

"So he was the one who was having the affair?"

"If the family stories are true, he was the one."

"Who was the woman?"

"I don't know. According to the commission papers like in your grandfather's stories, he also requested an encrypted message be etched on the back of the stones."

"What was the message?" I took the necklace off to show my father. "I've looked but haven't been able to find any message on these stones. What message are they talking about?"

"I'm assuming a love note to his lover."

I glanced back at the commission papers. I could see no note about a secret message. "Why isn't the message on the commission papers?"

"I doubt they wanted it written down on anything.

It would be dangerous, considering she was a married woman. Cousin to the czar or not, there could be a lot of political implications."

I put the necklace back on. I was wearing history. It must have been very difficult for Minna to give it up, not only because of the history but because it came from the love of her life. All the skeletons from the closet were coming out, rattling their bones, but I couldn't understand what they were trying to tell me. For now they'd have to wait. I had to get Kiri settled in. I'd talked to a local relief agency to see if they could place him with a foster family. A necessity. I glanced at my father who was gazing at Kiri through the window. I didn't want him to get too attached. My father or Kiri.

As my father and I went back in the rehab room, Kiri smiled at us. He walked along, hanging onto the railing. His whole life had changed in a matter of weeks. I could see the hope in his eyes. My father watched him, beaming. It reminded me that even though he loved me, that I must have been somewhat of a disappointment, not being a son, someone to carry on the Kustodia name.

Chapter Twelve

I sat in the back room of my father's store, studying the commission papers for the alexandrite necklace. I took the necklace off my neck. As my fingers ran along the cool stones, I felt the migraine starting. First a little dancing flash of light in the corner of my right eye followed by the swirling ceiling fans of light carried across to both eyes. And then the unbearable pounding in my head. I closed my eyes and took a deep breath. When I was a child, my parents had taken me to the top neurologists in Chicago. I'd been poked and tested, trying to find the source of these headaches. They called them flashing migraines or aura disturbance. Nothing in the scans showed a medical cause for the disturbance and what came after—the visions. The psychiatrist called them hallucinations. But to me they were real, brought on when I touched a stone with its own life. The doctors didn't believe me.

I'd held this necklace several times, never feeling the electricity. This time the surge of energy was the strongest I'd ever felt from any gem. It frightened me. I closed my eyes, the fluorescent light in the back office burning into my retinas. From the inside of my eyelids, a motion picture ran, a movie of a life I'd never lived—a time I'd never known. Gardenia. The overpowering sweet fragrance of gardenias filled the room. Violins. Cellos. It's a waltz. I hear a waltz. I opened my eyes. I was in the grand ballroom of the Winter Palace. Czar Nicholas was in his dress uniform; Alexandra was wearing a diamond-encrusted dress. They were leading the dance. The music sped up; the dancers twirled faster, faster. My head was pounding, the smell of gardenia making me nauseous. The music, faster and faster; their faces becoming a blur. The spinning ceiling fans. Their faces' skin peeling off, rotting flesh, soulless stares, the ballroom turning into a graveyard. The music becomes torturous screams. I dropped the necklace and covered my ears to stop the screaming. And then I was screaming.

"Alexandra," I heard. I felt somebody grab me.

I punched and screamed.

"Alexandra, Alexandra." My father pulled me into his arms and held me steady. I looked up into his face, afraid it would be the face of a corpse. "Alexandra, your headache? You're having your headache, aren't you?"

Then it stopped, and I collapsed in his arms. He carried me to the couch and brought me tea. "Drink this."

I sipped the tea, my hand shaking.

He came back with a glass of vodka. I downed it. "Father, the necklace; it's more than a love story."

"Alexandra, you just had one of your bad headaches. You hallucinate when you have those."

My father was more afraid of the headaches than I was. My mother had them and finally died from a brain tumor at age twenty-eight. I'm twenty-six. "It wasn't a hallucination. It was real. I could smell. I could taste."

My father sat next to me and took my hands in his. "Alexandra, your brain is lying to you. It's trying to fool you. All your senses are deceived. You're not yourself when these headaches happen."

After I cleared my head, I returned to the table

with the necklace. I placed it under the microscope. Peering down, I could make out the faint scratches on the backs of the stones. The scratches I'd seen before. I couldn't make out any writing or message. Fifty stones, none of them telling a story. I increased the magnification. With the LED light, the stones appeared more red than green. I thought about the story I'd heard a hundred times, about the love affair, the secret message, the rendezvous that never happened.

I sat back on the stool and switched off the light. Who were those people? What was their story? What was it about this woman that the Grand Duke would risk not just his political career for but his life? And why with all that at stake would he chance this beautiful necklace and a secret message? Why not just whisper the message in her ear as he held her under the Northern Lights?

Lights? My grandfather had said the message was visible only by candlelight. I searched the back room, opening drawers, rummaging through tools until I finally found a tall taper wedged in the back. I closed the door to the front and lit the candle. I turned off the lights. I placed the candle in the center of the necklace and slowly turned each stone like an old-fashioned Zoetrope. No animation came to life. I saw nothing other than scratches in the stones from a hundred years of wear. Maybe Minna had the answers. I blew out the candle and left.

When I arrived at Minna's building in Chicago's Gold Coast neighborhood, I waved to the doorman. He knew me from my years of visiting Minna and told me to go straight upstairs. I got in the elevator and pressed PH for penthouse. Her apartment occupied the entire fifteenth floor. I entered the small lobby off the elevator in front of her apartment. She had decorated it with a settee and a gilt table. Fresh flowers were brought in daily. Minna spared no expense when it came to beauty. As wealthy as she was, she was practical until it came to things of beauty—from flowers to gemstones. She appreciated perfection. I rang the doorbell adjacent to the door and waited a moment. Anxious to get answers, I knocked on the door, and it swung open. "Minna," I called, expecting to see her on the other side of the door. My only answer was silence. I entered the expansive living room, all gilt and gold and cream furnishings, its large picture window looking out on Chicago's Lake Michigan. Beautiful flowers in their nineteenth-century Russian silver gilt and cloisonné enamel vases hung wilted. A few vases were turned over and cracked. Magazines scattered on the white carpet.

"Minna!" I cried out. I walked down the long hallway toward her bedroom. All the drawers in her dressers were turned over and pulled out. Scraps of clothing lay across the floor. Her jewelry box had been upended and emptied onto the floor. I tripped over piles of pearls, diamonds and sapphires. Next to it, her *matroyshka* or Russian nesting dolls were tipped over, all torn apart. I picked one up and held it in my hand. Its face, the face of the Snow Queen, had cracked. She was smiling grotesquely. I'd played with these dolls as a girl. I glanced over at the stand by the window where Minna kept her special treasure, the Fabergé egg she'd brought with her from Russia. It was still in its place.

On the bed, her Louis Vuitton trunk lay open, half-filled, its contents spilling out onto the bed. I touched the silk scarf draped over its lid. I noticed her passport abandoned on top of the trunk. Packed in the pockets of it were photographs of my grandfather,

Minna's deceased sister, and me as a young girl. Minna had begun packing her memories but had never finished.

I went into her large walk-in closet. Same devastation but no sign of Minna anywhere. I fingered through the racks of clothes. Some had been wrenched from their hangers. By this late in the year, I'd have thought she would have had her furs out of cold storage, but there were none—not her blue sable, her Russian fox or her mink.

I sat on the bed and called my father. "I'm at Minna's. She's not here, the door was open, and her apartment's been torn apart."

"Get out of there. I'm calling the police," he said.

"I'm really worried about her." I sat on the bed and ran the scarf through my fingers. I didn't leave. I waited for the police. If it had been a burglary, why were none of her valuables taken? Her Fabergé egg, her jewelry, all were still here. When I had finished with the police, I returned to my father's apartment where he was waiting for me. He hugged me, handed me a cup of tea filled with vodka, our family remedy for anything and everything. "I spoke with the police," I said after I downed the tea. "They'll keep us informed. No other break-ins have been reported in the area. They filed a missing person's report but told me it wouldn't do much good. They're contacting local hospitals." I paused and sipped at my second cup of tea. "Have you spoken to Minna lately?"

"No, I've been busy with Kiri, your grandfather's estate, and the store. I did call her when you were in California after I cleared out your grandfather's safety deposit box. He included her in his will. You were also included."

"What was in the will?" I asked.

"He left Minna some uncut stones that she'd always admired and his silver tea service. He left you his Mercedes and the house," my father said, pouring me more tea.

"What am I going to do with the house?" I asked.

"You can sell it, or you can keep it. You can rent it. It doesn't matter. It's yours. It's paid off. The title was in the safety deposit box. He signed it over to you. It's in your name. I know he wanted to keep in it in the family. He hoped you'd have a family someday and live there."

A family—that was the furthest thought on my mind. "I'll clean it out and talk to a realtor." I could tell my father wasn't pleased with that answer. He had a lot on his plate, and so did I. The last thing I needed was a creaky old red brick farmhouse in downtown Oak Park, Illinois.

My thoughts turned back to Minna. "If someone broke into her apartment, where is she? Why didn't they take anything? Why wouldn't she have gone to the police? Why wouldn't she have come to us? I talked to her last night. She didn't mention anything about taking a trip, but it looked like she was packing and her passport was on the bed."

"I'll call her niece in Moscow to see if she's heard from her," my father said. The front door buzzer rang, and I looked at my father. "I forgot to tell you that while you were out I got a call from child services. There's a woman coming to see Kiri," he told me before walking out and down the stairs.

A few minutes later, he came back, followed by a woman flashing her DCFS badge. "Alexandra, this is Ms. Anderson. This is my daughter, Alexandra." The woman gave me a nod before sitting at the small kitchen table as my father poured her a cup of tea. Coming out of the bedroom, Kiri sat across from her.

My father sat next to Kiri. I could see his leg shaking.

The woman pulled out a notebook and jotted down notes. "Ms. Kustodia, I've been tasked to handle Kiri's file," she said. "There's a lot of missing information in the file about his circumstances and how he arrived in Chicago."

"Kiri's an orphan and needed medical attention," I said.

"Do you realize that by bringing him here you've skirted around all immigration and child safety laws? In most cases, we'd send the child back to Cambodia, but because of his therapy for his foot, we're going to allow him to stay in the country while we straighten this situation out."

"You have to understand..." I interrupted.

Ms. Anderson held her hand up. "I've dealt with Americans adopting internationally who've bent the laws in foreign countries using their political influence and bribing foreign officials, but Ms. Kustodia, that's not going to work here. I understand Mr. Carter has a lot of influence and I've been pressured to expedite Kiri's case, but I want to assure you, I'm going to do what is best for the child."

"Is it best to send him back to work clearing land mines for a drug lord? Starving and facing beatings? Is that what's best for this boy?" I said. My father reached over and placed his hand on my shoulder to calm me.

"There are thousands, millions of children in Kiri's situation around the world. It doesn't mean we can break the laws of our country and his. There's a right way to do this, and that's why I'm here."

At that point, I firmly grabbed my leg to stop myself from reaching across the kitchen table and strangling Ms. Anderson.

"Ms. Anderson." My father interrupted. "We all

want what's best for the boy. He can stay here while he's finishing his rehab and you file all the correct papers."

"I'm afraid that's not possible. You're not an approved foster home."

"What do we need to do to make us one?" my father asked.

"There has to be a home study, an evaluation, a background check. Becoming an approved foster home can take months, sometimes years."

"Nonsense; the boy's been living here for two months. We've got him the finest medical care, and I've registered him for school," my father said.

Kiri flipped his leg up onto the table to show off his new foot. "Ms. Anderson, ma'am, I can kick a soccer ball with this foot now. I'm getting very good. Do you want to see?"

She gave him a soft smile. "No, that's quite all right," she said. She stood up. "I'm afraid the boy's going to have to come with me until we get this straightened out."

Kiri looked to me and then to my father with horror. "Ms. Alex! Ms. Alex! Please don't let her take me!"

I could feel my bench-made blade rubbing against my thigh. I knew better. My father took Kiri's hand in his. "Boy, you need to go with Ms. Anderson. She'll take care of you. We'll straighten this out." I saw a look in my father's eye I hadn't seen before. It was fear. Fear for Kiri and what might happen to him. I sat quietly. My father gave Ms. Anderson a look. "Where will you take him? How quickly can we get a hearing?"

"We have a group facility in the suburbs that has an opening. He will be safe there. We'll make sure he makes his therapy appointments and keeps up with his schoolwork," she said, putting her notebook back in her briefcase.

"Kiri, get your things," I said. Kiri ran out of the room. When he returned, he was carrying the backpack and the soccer ball my father had given him. I knelt down and whispered in his ear, "I will come for you, I promise." I handed him a piece of paper with my cell phone number. He hugged me tightly and then turned and clung to my father. My father ruffled his hair. "Go now, boy." Unable to watch, he turned away from the door as Kiri and Ms. Anderson left.

I left the room before Kiri did. I went into my old bedroom and paced up and down, clenching my fists. I grabbed my boot knife and flung it against the wall, sticking it dead on. I could hear my father in the other room on the phone, speaking in Russian.

I went back out into the kitchen. My father was sitting at the table, a glass in his hand. He had switched his tea to vodka. He filled half a water glass and slid it over to me.

I took a gulp straight from the bottle. "What are we going to do about Minna? Did you call her niece in Moscow?"

"Yes. She hasn't heard from her."

"Aren't you worried?"

"Wherever Minna is, she's fine. She's traveled around the world. She can take care of herself."

Hunter snuggled around my leg. Neither my father nor I spoke of Kiri. I tried calling Carter. He's the one who'd started this whole mess, but his phone went to voicemail. He'd gotten what he wanted, and I had a feeling he was done with me.

It was almost midnight when I went to my bedroom. I switched out of my jeans and put on my old T-shirt I'd left in the closet. I climbed into bed before Hunter could beat me to the pillow. Gem lay at my feet, purring. I lay on my back staring at the ceiling, thinking about Minna, thinking about Kiri. Then my phone vibrated. I reached over to the nightstand. I didn't recognize the number. There was static, and then a voice cut through, a heavily accented voice.

"Alex," Erik said from the other end of the line.

"Erik, where are you?"

"I'm at O'Hare."

"What are you doing in Chicago?"

"Minna called me a few days ago. I was in Thailand. All she said was it's urgent I fly to Chicago, and she'd pick me up. I haven't been able to reach her."

"I'll come get you." I quickly pulled my jeans on and slipped into my shoes. I grabbed the keys to my father's car. There was no traffic heading west on I-90 out to O'Hare. The Porsche Cayenne easily did a hundred and ten miles an hour. It felt like I was barely moving. I pulled in front of arrivals at international terminal five. I saw the big Swede standing at the curb with his backpack, smoking a cigar. He was wearing cargo shorts and a T-shirt, oblivious to the thirty-seven-degree temperature. I pulled up in front of him and lowered the passenger window.

He stuck his head in and said, "*Tack sa mycket*."

"You're welcome," I replied.

He threw his backpack on the floor and jumped into the passenger seat.

I gave him a glance, and he knew to put his cigar out. He opened the window and flicked it out. His broad shoulders stretched across his seat, brushing against me. It wasn't an unpleasant feeling, just the opposite. "Where's Minna?" he asked.

I glanced over quickly as I drove back out to the city. "She's gone."

"What do you mean she's gone? She asked me to fly here."

"She's gone. I went to her apartment, and it was torn apart. It looked like she'd been packing when someone broke in."

"What about the police?"

"They were going to check the area hospitals and put out a missing person's report."

"I've known Minna for twenty years, and I've never heard her as nervous as she was on the phone."

Twenty years, I thought. I would have been six years old. I didn't think he was that old. "You never told me how you met Minna."

"When I was a boy, we met at the diamond show in Antwerp. My father was a diamond dealer in Stockholm. He brought me with him to the annual diamond show. He wanted to teach me the trade. I wasn't much more than twelve or thirteen. After meeting her, my father commissioned Minna to hunt for blue diamonds in South Africa."

The Heart of Eternity, a twenty-seven-carat fancy vivid blue diamond, was discovered in South Africa. "I've seen the Heart of Eternity at the Field Museum in Chicago," I said.

"The mine where it was found is where Minna went. She took me with her. My father paid her to take me so I could learn gem hunting. I spent six weeks with Minna, searching for blue diamonds. That was my first snakebite—a spitting cobra. Minna nursed me back to health. We've had many adventures since then. She knows that I'll come when she calls, but she wouldn't take me away from a paying job unless it was urgent."

"You can stay with me and my father tonight. In

the morning, we can figure this out," I said and then yawned.

He turned and stared at me, watching me drive. It made me uncomfortable but in a good way. I cracked my window. He laid his head back on the headrest and closed his eyes. I glanced over and watched his chest move up and down as he breathed. His long blond beard danced with every inhale, every exhale. Any image I'd ever had of a Viking would have included this man sleeping next to me. I lowered my window to let more cold air in.

When we arrived, I unlocked the door to my father's apartment, quietly so as not to wake him. As I opened the door, Hunter sat staring at me and my companion. He'd caught my scent even before I'd entered the building. He ran up to Erik and circled him, sniffing cautiously. He could sense I was at ease, so he became at ease. Erik reached down to try to pet Hunter, but he wouldn't have it. Gem on the other hand became fast friends and flipped over on her back as Erik rubbed her furry belly. I hadn't pictured Erik as a cat or dog person. *Wolf*, maybe? "You can take my room. I'll sleep on the couch," I said, pointing down the hall.

"No, I don't want to put you out." He adjusted his backpack on his shoulder.

"It's better you're behind a closed door, otherwise Hunter will be pacing all night."

"Thank you," Erik said, touching my arm. Hunter let out a low growl. "I see what you mean." Erik wandered off in the direction I'd pointed, pulling off his T-shirt as he walked.

He passed under the moonlight cascading through the skylight above the living room. As he did, I noticed for the first time the scars on his back. Long healed-over welts resembling whiplashes tattooed his back. I grabbed the bottle of Ketel One from the freezer, didn't bother with a glass, and sat on the couch. Hunter and Gem joined me. My uncomplicated life had just gotten very complicated.

Chapter Thirteen

The clatter of coffee mugs slamming onto the table woke me up. I sat up, rubbing at my eyes and stretching my arms. Erik sat at the table, a fresh cup of coffee in his hand. Both my father and Erik kept staring over at me. "Alexandra, it's about time you woke up. You want to introduce me to your friend?" my father asked.

I stood up and walked to the table. "Father, this is Erik. Erik, this is my father, Peter." I sat on a chair and reached for a coffee mug. I filled it and stirred in cream. I avoided both of their gazes.

Erik nodded. My father continued clanging around the kitchen, banging plates and silverware onto the table. He placed scrambled eggs, black bread toast and jam onto the table and then sat down with a thud. Erik dug in like he hadn't eaten in days. I sipped my coffee. My father sat glaring at me, waiting to hear the story.

"Erik Helmstrom; he was my guide in Cambodia. I told you Minna connected me with him. He has a history with her."

"Why is he here?"

Erik looked up, picking scrambled eggs out of his beard.

"He called me last night from O'Hare. Minna was supposed to pick him up, but she never showed." I paused. "Father, I'm worried about Minna. She called Erik, saying it was urgent he fly to Chicago. She's not at her apartment; none of her family in Russia has heard from her. Now Erik is sitting here with no idea why she called him."

"I'll make some calls. Perhaps you can go to Russian Tea Time and ask Katrina if they've seen her. Let's finish our breakfast. I have to open the shop." My father ate quickly. "I'm meeting with Mr. Markey this afternoon about Kiri. His firm handles immigration issues. He's done work for friends of the family."

"How is Kiri? Where is he?" Erik asked.

"He's been fitted with a prosthetic foot and has been doing great with his therapy. We're trying to find a family to place him with. He was staying with us until child services took him and put him in a group home," I said.

"I don't understand. You took this boy out of the ghettos of Cambodia, paid his medical bills and gave him a home, and the United States government took him away?"

I shook my head. "That's how things work here. I know it doesn't make any sense."

"What about your big-shot movie star? This is all his doing. He doesn't have any political power here? Even in Thailand people know his name."

"I haven't been able to reach him." I had Carter's number on speed dial and had dialed it repeatedly.

Erik took out his phone and typed something in. He flipped over the screen and showed me pictures of Carter filming a movie in Vancouver. It was an article in *People*. Carter's arm was draped around a different girl than the one I'd seen him with at the premiere. "It doesn't help. He's not answering his phone. I don't have any other way to get in touch with him."

"I flew fourteen hours, two flights to get here; what's another four hours?"

"You want to fly to Vancouver, break onto the set and get Hollywood's biggest action hero to take a break from his one-hundred-million-dollar movie to help us get an eight-year-old refugee boy out of a group home?"

"That pretty much sums it up. I'd say this guy owes us, and I've got nowhere else to be." Erik leaned back in his chair.

I looked at my father, who nodded and said, "You two go see Mr. Carter. I'll call Katrina and ask around about Minna. You work on getting Kiri back home."

I grabbed my passport and backpack while Erik called and made flight reservations.

Chapter Fourteen

A few hours later, Erik and I stood in the entrance of a converted warehouse, reading the sign out front: Tom Carter, *Blood Tea*. Carter's assistant had gotten us onto the closed set and told us to stay back and keep quiet. I shifted my weight on my foot as Erik and I watched Carter. I had wanted to barge in and announce our presence, but Erik stopped me. Carter appeared to be taking tea-drinking lessons.

"Like this?" Carter asked, holding his pinky out as he balanced a tiny teacup in his hand.

"No, more like this." A woman demonstrated as she moved Carter's hand so his pinky stuck out at a more pronounced angle.

"Shit!" Carter exclaimed as the tea poured all over him.

The woman dabbed at Carter's clothes with a napkin. I shifted my feet again and decided I'd waited long enough. "Carter!" I called out, stepping across the studio stage that separated us.

At the sound of my voice, he spilled the remaining tea on his white ruffled shirt. He waved me off and then ran off to his trailer parked outside the large warehouse doors. The woman walked to the concession table that was piled high with sandwiches, bagels, and fruit.

"Excuse me," I said. "I need to talk to Tom Carter."

"I'm just the tea wrangler. You have to talk to one of the assistant directors. I'm sure the wardrobe people are helping Mr. Carter change. By the way, my name is Karen Owen."

"Tea wrangler? I don't think I've ever heard of that title before." I exchanged amused glances with Erik.

"Actually, I'm not a tea wrangler. I own a tea shop here in Vancouver. They were scouting locations. When they saw my tea shop, they asked me to be a consultant on the movie. I deal with exotic teas and antique teacups."

"Why does Carter need a tea wrangler?"

Karen smiled. "The movie's called *Blood Tea*. It's the story behind the Boston Tea Party and the politics involved with the tea party in colonial America."

"So you have to teach Tom Carter how to drink tea?"

She smiled again. "There are some nuances to seeping and drinking tea from that era. He wants everything to be very authentic. From what I understand, he wants all his movies to be as realistic as possible. He wants the viewer to be transported."

I understood what she was saying after spending time with him in the jungles of Cambodia. That had been a very authentic experience. Karen waved to one of the men circling around Carter's trailer. He walked over to us. "I'm sorry. I didn't get your name," he said.

"I'm Alex Kustodia. I've done some work with Tom Carter. You might call us friends."

"I'm the assistant director, Michael Cummings." He scanned the list he was holding on a clipboard. "I don't have you on the set list. You're going to have to leave."

I glanced around the soundstage at the hundred or so people flicking around like fireflies. All here to make one particular action hero look good. I thought about Kiri back home, how one phone call from Carter could change his life. When the assistant director left, I thanked Karen the tea wrangler and headed over to the trailer. Jake, his bodyguard, stood watch over the door and held out his arm to stop me. When he recognized me, he gave me a smile and waved me in. Erik followed me into the trailer. Carter was in a downward dog yoga position. Hearing the door open, he looked over the back of his shoulder. "Alex. Was that you before? I didn't recognize you. I'm doing some stretching before the next scene." He turned around again when Erik walked in, nearly bumping his head on the trailer door. "Oh, Erik, right? Are you guys a thing now or something?"

"No, he's helping me with Kiri," I said.

Carter switched to the lotus position. He motioned out his trailer window to the tea wrangler who flew in the door. "I need something to mellow me out. Something maybe orangey, fruity, and put some MCT oil in it."

Karen looked at me and gave a smile of recognition that Carter was an idiot before she left again.

"Kiri? Kiri?" A look of understanding dawned on his face. "That's the little cripple from Cambodia, right? I thought his name was Kevin."

I sighed. "No, it's Kiri. He's been staying with me. He's been fitted with a prosthetic foot, and he's going through physical therapy. Social services took him away."

Carter stood in warrior position. "Why'd they take him away?"

"We brought him into the country illegally. We didn't complete the proper paperwork. We have an immigration attorney working on it. In the meantime, they stuck him in some children's home."

"Prosthetic foot, huh? That's a good idea."

"Yeah, it's a good idea."

"What I mean is, I got a lot of play out of the Cambodia trip. I launched my charity, *Give a Hand, Give a Foot*. I remember there were a lot of crippled kids in the village like…"

"Kiri, yes, a lot of children lost limbs, clearing land mines. That's still going on." I nodded.

"This is something I can work with. I have to get a hold of my publicist and my manager. Kiri can be our poster child. We can use him to raise money for my charity. It's all about the kids." He went into eagle arms.

Karen entered the trailer again, balancing a tray that held a delicate china teacup. "This is a Meissen teacup and saucer. It's from 1745. Can you please be careful? It's worth about fifteen hundred."

Carter knocked into the tray, sending the teacup wobbling. He reached out and grabbed it before it hit the ground. "Sorry, trying to stay in character," he said.

I had nothing to say.

He sipped his tea and went to place the cup on the edge of his table. It fell and shattered. Karen gasped and ran out of the trailer. "Let me make some phone calls about Kevin. I might want to fly him out to the set for a photo op. Do you think we could make that happen?" Carter asked.

"If you get him out of the home, we can make it happen," I agreed.

"Great. This will be great. I'll get my people on it." Carter walked over the broken china pieces to the door of his trailer. He gave me a big hug. My chin rested on the top of his head. Erik gave him a nod. We left the trailer, closing the door behind us.

"So what do you think? Will he make this

happen?" Erik asked.

"It's to his benefit, so I think he will," I said as we reached the rental car. "I could use a beer."

We found a little restaurant on the edge of Stanley Park overlooking the expansive forest and the sea. Erik finished six fish tacos and five pints of Guinness. We sat quietly, watching the beautiful scenery. "It reminds me of the time I spent in Sweden. The ocean, the forest, the mountains," I said.

"Yes, but it's very warm here for late fall."

I checked the weather app on my iPhone. It was thirty-eight degrees. I smiled. "Where do you think Minna could be?"

"I have no idea. I emailed several of my friends whom she's worked with—either dealers or bush pilots. No one's heard from her."

"Did she give any indication of what she wanted when she asked you to come to Chicago?"

"She said she needed to get out of the country and that was it."

"She didn't say anything else? If she needed to leave the country, why wouldn't she just hop a plane at O'Hare? Why wouldn't she call me? Why wouldn't she tell us she was leaving? None of this makes any sense." So many lingering questions. We had no answers for any of them. I ran my hand through my hair, pulling it back into a ponytail.

"Don't take it personal. I know you're very close to Minna, and she's very close to you. She's spoken of you many times on our different trips. I know she loved you."

I grabbed his arm. "*Love*, not loved. Don't talk about her like she's dead." I shuddered. I could hear my grandmother's voice. Maybe that was one Russian superstition I believed in.

We paid at the register, walked outside, and

strolled along the expansive seawall.

"Minna had... *has* many friends, people who love her. She's also made many enemies over the years, including drug lords and gangsters. Government officials. She's worked around the law to get what she wanted," Erik said.

"Yes, I know all that. I've done similar things myself when I've needed to." There were several instances that immediately came to mind, including my excursion to India.

"Minna may have done some questionable things, but she's also helped many people. She saved the lives of many families escaping Bosnia," Erik said.

"I didn't know any of this. I knew about her gem trading. I didn't know about her activism. She never talked about that."

"No, she wouldn't. She probably wanted to protect you from it. Are you familiar with the lost boys of Sudan?"

I shook my head.

"Back in the late 1980s during the second Sudanese war, a couple million people were killed. Millions were displaced. The title *lost boys* was given to the boys in the refugee camps. Those boys, usually orphans, were fleeing the violence in southern Sudan. They had nothing—no food, no possessions. The soldiers hunted them down to enlist them. The boys made their way into Ethiopia and Kenya. Minna was hunting diamonds in Ethiopia at the time. She heard about the refugees and organized a group of local villagers, relief workers, and got thousands of children safely out of Sudan. But by doing that, she also angered the LRA—the Lord's Resistance Army, an active militant group in southern Sudan. That's where the scars on my back came from. I saw you notice them last night at your apartment. Minna and I were captured by the LRA in 1998. Minna hired me to fly her into southern Sudan to meet with a dealer who had a new mine of sapphires. He was working for the LRA and gave Minna over to them. She was beaten to the point of near death. That's why she limps today. I was thrown into a pit for a week. If it weren't for the fact that we were worth so much ransom, they would have killed us. These are the people who Minna has in her past—the kind of people who wouldn't hesitate to kill her."

"Why would they come after her now? She's an old woman. She hasn't left Chicago in the past ten years."

"I don't know. Minna has always looked over her shoulder. Maybe her past has finally caught up to her. I think when we get back to Chicago we should check out her apartment again to see if there's anything you missed."

We reached the edge of the forest and stood looking out over the bay. The water was a brilliant blue, the color of the rarest blue zircon. The setting sun smeared across the cobalt sky like a lipstick kiss. The temperature dropped. I pulled my North Face windbreaker tight around my neck.

"Are you cold?" Erik asked with a surprised look. He was not wearing anything other than a flannel shirt and jeans. He put his arm around me so I could feel the warmth of his chest against mine. As he pulled me closer, I suddenly felt a searing pain tear across my left arm, and then I heard the gunshot. Erik heard it too and pulled me down to the ground.

The two of us rolled under some evergreen bushes, Erik's body protectively covering mine. I pushed him away. "Where'd that come from?" I asked. "I felt it before I heard it."

Erik was busy checking me out to make sure I

wasn't hit anywhere else. "It grazed your skin. It was a nick." He tore up his flannel and pushed it against my wound. "It's still bleeding a lot. Hold this tight. It must have been pretty far away for us to hear the gunfire a second later. A high-powered rifle from up in the mountains." We both peered through the evergreens but didn't see anything. There was no other sound, no movement. Nothing. "We have to stay here until dark," Erik said.

About a half hour later, the woods were as dark as obsidian. We made it back to the walkway that traversed into the small town and checked into a quaint seaside bed-and-breakfast. Erik had wanted to take me to the hospital, but I refused. Instead, I lay on the bed. Erik left and returned shortly with gauze, peroxide, and bandages. He pulled my long-sleeve shirt over my head. The bleeding had mostly stopped, but my bra was soaked with blood. "This is going to sting a bit." He rubbed the peroxide on to clean it. "You'll have a bit of a scar but not much." He went back into the bag he'd retrieved and handed me a Vancouver T-shirt. "I thought you might need a change of clothes."

I went into the bathroom and got undressed. I took a shower and put on the extra-large T-shirt. I walked out of the bathroom, drying my hair, dabbing at the tips with the towel. Erik sat in the overstuffed reading chair by the window. He had closed the blinds. He poured us each a glass of vodka.

I sat on the edge of the bed next to him and downed four ounces. He nodded at me and said, "*Ska*," and did the same. My arm ached slightly. "What just happened?" I asked. "Who'd want to kill me? Who even knows we're here?"

"I think we should call the police." Erik refilled our glasses.

The vodka burning my throat eased the pain in my arm. "No, I have to leave in the morning. I have to get back to my dad and Kiri. I have to find Minna. Besides, what are we going to tell them? We didn't see where the shot came from. I don't know who'd want to kill me. I don't even know if they were shooting at me. It could have been random."

"It was only one shot. A high-powered rifle and it hit your arm. If you hadn't been moving at the time, it would have gone right for your heart. Whoever it was, was aiming for you." Erik downed his glass and refilled it.

I sat back on the bed and said, "My grandfather was murdered. Then Minna disappears. The only connection to both is me."

"When we get back to Chicago, we'll look at Minna's apartment. For now, let's get some sleep. I'll take the couch, you can have the bed," Erik said.

I glanced at the small five-foot Victorian-era couch, and then I looked at the very large Erik Helmstrom. "We can share the bed. It's fine." I jumped in and pulled the down comforter over me. I was exhausted.

Erik filled his glass, downed it again, and went into the bathroom. I heard the shower running. I turned off the light next to the bed as I listened to the water hitting the shower floor. When he stepped in, I could hear it pounding off his body. I closed my eyes. The shower stopped. The room was dark except for the slices of moonlight coming through the slats of the blinds. I could make out Erik's outline as he walked back into the bedroom, wearing a towel. Then as he reached his side of the bed, the towel came off. I tried to sleep, but sleep wouldn't come. I could hear his heart beating next to me. Then I realized it was my heart pounding. Erik was sound asleep. I drifted off.

Chapter Fifteen

Erik and I arrived at the store at lunchtime. I'd picked up hot dogs for my father and us. He greeted us at the front door, holding it wide open.

"Alex, come in." He nodded at Erik. There was a new face standing behind the counter, a young woman I didn't recognize. "Alex, this is Amy. She's a licensed gemologist. She's helping out with all the new clients. The publicity from the ruby necklace has overwhelmed the store. I can't keep up with all the orders that have come in."

I nodded at Amy as she spoke on the phone and waved to me.

"Come in the back." My father led us to the back room. We sat at the small table. "I spoke with the attorney about Kiri. He's been in contact with social services. Even better, your trip to Vancouver was a success. Early this morning, Mr. Carter's people pulled some strings."

"What do you mean?" I asked, emptying the bag onto the table. I brought over paper plates and ketchup.

"We've been invited out to the children's home this afternoon to bring Kiri back home with us. Carter's on his way here to do some kind of presentation to the home. Something about helping hands, helping feet. I don't know what it means."

I smiled as my father continued, "At first I didn't understand what the attorney was saying. According to him, I've been named a foster home and they're going to release Kiri to me until they can find a permanent home for him. That's the good news. He can stay with me. At least he's out of that place and back here where he belongs."

I hadn't seen my father this excited about anything in a long time. Since my mother had died, his life had been all about the store. I hadn't been around much. I took off my jacket and sat down to eat.

"Alexandra, your arm? What happened to your arm?" my father asked, staring at the bandage poking out the bottom of the T-shirt sleeve.

"It's nothing. I scratched it on the movie set. They were doing a stunt, and I got in the way."

"Let me see."

"Father, it's fine. Erik cleaned it and taped it up."

"Erik fixed your arm?"

Erik pulled hot dog crumbs out of his beard, not paying attention.

I wanted to change the subject. "When do we pick up Kiri?"

"We have to leave for Woodstock in a half hour. That's where the home is, and it'll take us a while to get there."

"Any word about Minna? Did you speak with Katrina at the tearoom?"

My father downed his fourth hot dog and drank down his Coke. "Yes, Minna called her. Katrina said she sounded worried. Minna told her she was leaving town. That's all she said. Katrina and Minna have been friends for forty years. If there was more to the story, she would have told Katrina, and Katrina would have told me. All she said was that Minna sounded worried and that's not like Minna."

"Erik and I are going to her apartment to see if we can find any clues as to where she went." I threw away the fast-food wrappings.

"After Woodstock though," my father said, "we have to leave. I want you to be there when they release Kiri. He will want to see you."

"Father, I'm worried that he's getting too attached to us. This is a temporary solution. He needs a real family. A father, a mother, a house in the suburbs, a dog."

"This boy was living in the mud, scrounging through garbage in Cambodia. You don't think my apartment's better than that? You don't think I'm better than that?" My father pounded the table with his fist.

"Don't get angry. I'm more worried that you're getting attached."

He finished his last hot dog and didn't say a word.

We drove along the Illinois flatland corridor known as I-90 to the far northwestern suburb of Woodstock. We turned onto the long tree-lined driveway that had once been some meatpacking magnate's summer home. He'd donated it to the state, and they'd turned it into this group home. As we pulled up to the front of the building, we saw a line of limousines. Paparazzi greeted us, snapping pictures. When we got out of the car, they seemed disappointed. We made our way through the crowd to the top of the stairs to the old English manor home with ivy crawling up the side. Our attorney was waiting for us. He shook my father's hand and led us into the building. Inside was more spectacle, and at the center of it was Tom Carter. He flashed his fifty-thousand-watt smile at me.

"Alex!" He ran over and gave me a big hug. "Great, you made it. Erik." He hugged Erik, getting lost in Erik's chest, lingering uncomfortably long for both Erik and for me. "And Mr. Kustodia?" He hugged my father. "Everything is set. We're going to do a little presentation, give a check to the home, announce the formation of the *Give a Hand, Give a Foot* charity foundation."

"Where's Kiri?" I asked.

"Who?"

"Kiri."

"Oh, Kevin. He's in the office with my publicist and my administrator. They're coaching him on what to say."

"Great." I nodded.

Karen Owen, the tea wrangler, walked up behind Carter and handed him a stainless steel travel mug. Carter took a sip and spit it out. "What's this?"

"It's an herbal tea to calm your nerves: a little organic honey, St. John's wort, and a few other medicinals."

"I don't want to be calm. I want to be the opposite of calm. I want to be uncalm. Get me something with extra caffeine." He handed her the mug and stormed off.

"Karen, do you travel with Carter now?" I asked.

She pulled me to the side and whispered, "Yeah, the studio hired me to be his tea consultant and herbalist."

"Really?"

"I don't understand it either, but the pay's really good. I get to travel and I get to buy some amazing tea."

Kiri walked out of the office, followed by two women, the first one dressed in a pencil skirt and cotton sweater. The other, who I assumed was Carter's publicist, was wearing a very expensive power suit. The publicist motioned for Karen to bring her a tea. She clapped her hands together to get everyone's attention and said, "Hi, everybody; we're going to head out front. Tom's going to say a few words about the charity, hug the boy, Kevin."

"Kiri, the boy's name is Kiri," I corrected her.

"Yes, Kiri. Take a couple of questions from the crowd. We'd like to introduce you and your father and so on."

We opened the front door as cameras clicked and lights flashed. Hidden by the brick rail that circled the porch, I saw a small wooden box that Carter climbed up on. I followed him, standing behind him.

"Hello, everybody! Thanks for coming out. I feel that it's my responsibility—no, make that my duty—as a human being to give back, to take care of, to make better the lives of those less fortunate. It's all about the children," Carter exclaimed. The cameras clicked; the news crews shot video. "I'd like to introduce you to this wonderful young man who I rescued from the ghettos of the Cambodian jungles and the warlords." The publicist pushed Kiri out onto the landing. I knelt down next to him. He gave me a hug and a kiss.

"This is Kiri. He's eight years old. Like thousands of his friends back in Cambodia, he was injured. He lost his foot, clearing landmines for the ruthless crime lords and smugglers. His life was a nightmare, living day to day, begging for scraps, eating garbage. And now." The publicist tapped Kiri on the shoulder. Kiri took his gym shoe off. "Now he's got a foot up on the rest of the kids," Carter said while Kiri showed the crowd his prosthetic foot. The publicist reached back and grabbed his soccer ball. Kiri bounced it off his knee and foot, back and forth. "Now he has a foot. He has a home, and most of all, he has hope. All it took was a hand and a foot. That's why I named my charity: *Give a Hand, Give a Foot.* We want to help other children not just in Cambodia but around the world who have lost limbs."

The crowd applauded. Carter knelt down next to Kiri for pictures, hugging him, holding up the soccer ball, smiling.

Carter took questions, flashing his smile, while my father and I gathered up Kiri, his belongings, and left, heading back to Chicago. During the whole ride back to Chicago, Kiri talked about his time with Carter, about how he was going to be on the cover of magazines and visit him in Hollywood.

"The lady at the home said I would be living with you, Miss Alex," he said.

"Not me, Kiri, but they said you can stay for the time being with my father."

"Pappa?"

"Yes, you'll be staying with my father in his apartment until we find you a real home."

Kiri grew silent and rolled his soccer ball in his hands. During the remainder of the forty-minute ride, he didn't say a word.

We dropped my father and Kiri off. I gathered up Hunter and Gem before heading back to the car. We drove the few blocks to my apartment. I hadn't been home in weeks. It already didn't feel like home. The management office was scheduling the closing. All I had left to do was pack my belongings and hand over my keys.

Erik parked the car while I walked Hunter. We headed to the sixtieth floor together and walked down the narrow hallway leading to my end unit. I stopped when I got to the door, unlocking it. We stepped in. I released Gem from her carrier. Hunter ran around the apartment, sniffing and growling. "Easy, boy," I said.

"What's wrong with him?"

"He was like this the day before I left for Cambodia. Like something wasn't right." I looked around, scanning the room. Everything was in its place as far as I remembered. I went into the bedroom. Everything there looked right. Hunter paced back and forth in front of the floor vent under the windows. He scratched at the floor around the vent, growling. "What is it, Hunter? What are you doing? You're scratching my floor."

Erik knelt down, and taking out his pocket knife, he unscrewed the vent cover and turned it over. He turned around to me and held his finger to his lips. He flipped over the cover, revealing a tiny metal magnet no larger than a dime. Before I could speak, he stopped me. He put the vent cover back down and grabbed a pen off my writing desk and wrote on a scrap of paper. "That's a listening device."

"Why?" I mouthed.

He shook his head. He didn't know. I didn't know. He took my hand and led me into the bathroom. He turned on the faucet and the shower. "There may be more around the apartment. We'll have to get a debugger to find all the listening devices."

"But why? Who? How long have they been here?"

"I'm guessing that whoever shot at you in Vancouver planted these listening devices and took Minna. Whatever you and Minna know, someone is willing to kill for it."

As I stood listening to Erik, I ran my fingers along the alexandrite necklace. The necklace had become my rosary. I hadn't taken it off since the funeral. "Erik, my necklace! Minna gave this to me the day of my grandfather's funeral. There was a man at the gravesite back in the woods watching us."

Erik ran his finger along the curves of the necklace, lifting it gently off my chest. "It's beautiful," he whispered, still gazing at my chest.

"There's a whole family history behind it. We can't talk here."

I took one last look around the apartment, filled a backpack with some clothes and what little jewelry I kept here and my two most precious possessions, Hunter and Gem.

We drove to my grandfather's house. I didn't want to disturb my father. I was worried that I'd lead whoever was following me to Kiri and my father. I couldn't risk that. As I opened the door, I turned to Erik. "This was my grandfather's house. He left it to me." We walked into the house, which smelled musty like it hadn't been aired out in a while. I felt uneasy; I could feel my grandfather's presence, his ghost. This house was always a home to me, and whatever evil was done here wasn't going to change that. Wasn't going to change all the love I felt growing up here. The key to finding his killer was hidden somewhere in this house.

I led Erik down the staircase off the kitchen that led into the full basement where my grandfather kept his lapidary lab. I turned on the overhead light.

Erik looked around at all the cutting and polishing tools, some of them over a hundred years old.

"These were my great-grandfather's. He brought them with him from Russia." I took the necklace off and placed it under the fluorescent light on the workbench. The stones turned a reddish hue.

"It's beautiful alexandrite," Erik said, leaning over my shoulder.

"My great-grandfather mined these stones in the Ural Mountains in the early 1900s. He created this necklace. According to the family story, the Grand Duke Ferdinand Romanov, cousin of the czar, commissioned my great-grandfather to create this necklace for his secret love, a married woman. My father just recently found the actual commission paper in my grandfather's safety deposit box. The duke had my great-grandfather inscribe a message to his love on the stones."

I watched Erik pick up the necklace and hold it up to the fluorescent light. "You can see it better by candlelight." I lit a candle and pulled the chain on the workshop light over the bench. I handed Erik a loupe and studied him as he turned it slowly in the candlelight. "It's just a bunch of scratches. It's worn off," I said, looking over his shoulder.

He examined the stones closely, studying each one. "These aren't scratches. There's a pattern—dot dot dash—It's Morse code."

I took the loupe from his hand and gazed closer at the stones. I'd been looking for Russian or English letters. All I saw were a bunch of scratches. Was this the secret love letter?

Erik grabbed a pen and a pad of paper and handed it to me. "Write this down." He took the necklace back and started reading off the code. "North 56.83333 and east 60.5833."

"What is that?" I asked.

"It's latitude and longitude." Erik took out his iPhone and typed in the numbers. "It's the town of Ekaterinburg."

"That makes sense. That's where the Grand Duke lived, and that's where my great-grandfather's shop was. What's the rest?"

"The next are letters. Write this down. That's *d-e-a-d*."

"Dead," I repeated, staring at the letters as I wrote them down.

"*Will live*," Erik finished reading. "*Dead will live*."

"Dead will live," I repeated. "What does that mean? That's not very romantic."

"You said Grand Duke? Was this before the revolution?"

"Yes."

"We should find out more about this Grand Duke," Erik said, handing the necklace back to me.

"I researched him after my father gave me the commission paper, but it's all pretty much the same Wikipedia stuff—some true, some fairy tales about the Romanovs. There's one person who can tell us more. She was a professor of Russian history and owns the Russian tearoom. She can trace her family back to before imperial Russia," I said.

We looked at each other. "Let's go," Erik said. While only a few miles, the traffic down 290 was punishing in the midafternoon. It took almost two hours to get to the South Loop where the tearoom was located.

We took a table in the back. The waitress came over to take our order. "Is Katrina here? Would you tell her Alexandra would like to see her?" I asked.

A short while later, a round, jolly, dark-haired woman in a colorful peasant dress, who resembled a Russian nesting doll, walked over to the table. I stood to greet her. She squeezed me tight.

"Alexandra, is good to see you. I was so sorry to hear about your grandfather." I nodded my appreciation, not saying a word. "And who is this fine man?"

Erik stood towering over her while she hugged him about the waist and lingered a while as apparently most people who hug Erik like to do. "Oh, Alexandra, he's beautiful!" Katrina gave an approving nod to me.

"He's a friend," I replied. "Erik Helmstrom."

Katrina took another look. "Yes, Mr. Helmstrom, Minna has spoken about you many times. She never mentioned how handsome you are." She squeezed his arm. "And how strong you are."

"Erik, Katrina is one of Minna's oldest friends."

"Yes, that's right. We both came to the United States in the 1960s." She sat down and waved the waitress over to bring the tea samovar. She spoke rapidly in Russian. The waitress hurried over with black currant tea, plum strudel, sugar cookies and raisin scones with fresh clotted cream.

Erik ate half the plate with relish, gulping his tea in between bites. I nibbled at the plum strudel. "Katrina, my father said he spoke to you about Minna."

"Yes, yes, I have not heard from her since the day she called. I called friends and family in Russia and some of her neighbors on the Gold Coast. I even called Father John at Holy Trinity. He has not seen her since church service. No one has seen her."

"Katrina, if you hear from Minna, can you let us know? We're very worried about her."

"Of course, but for now let's enjoy our company," Katrina said.

"Do you know the story of Grand Duke Ferdinand Romanov and my great-grandfather?"

"Yes." Katrina nodded. "Any good Russian knows the story of the duke's secret romance."

"My grandfather never said who the duke's lover was."

Katrina began, "According to legend, she was a general's wife, and according to stories I heard as a little girl, the general was a traitor to the imperial family. He was one of the spies plotting the revolution and the assassination of the Romanovs. The Grand Duke being the czar's cousin was loyal to the imperial family and supposedly gained the aid of the general's wife as a spy gathering information."

As Katrina spoke, I rubbed the necklace. She stopped and looked. "Is that the necklace, the necklace from the story? Is that why you're asking about the Grand Duke?"

"Yes, this is the necklace from all our childhood stories. My great-grandfather made this necklace for the Grand Duke. My grandfather searched for it for years. He gave it to Minna, then she gave it to me at his funeral. There was a message inscribed on the back of the necklace from the Grand Duke to his love. It's a location and the words, 'The dead shall live.'"

"The dead shall live," Katrina repeated.

"Is that some sort of Russian saying that didn't translate correctly? Do you know what that means?"

"According to the story, before the Romanovs were taken into custody, the czarina tasked the Grand Duke with smuggling priceless treasures out of Russia—seven caskets worth. The last fortune of the Romanovs. The caskets were never found."

"The dead shall live."

Katrina laughed a hearty laugh, creaking back on her chair. "My dear little Malenkaya. So many have tried through the centuries to find the lost treasure of the Romanovs. Believe me, it was scattered throughout the world if it even left Russia. That's a fool's journey you don't want to take. Minna and I spent many late nights, drinking, laughing, and telling the old stories of the seven caskets."

We finished our tea. Erik reached into his pocket to pull out his wallet. "No, this is on me," Katrina said. "Let's have a toast!" She motioned over to the waitress. The waitress brought over a flight of flavor-infused vodkas. "This is called a flight of jewels. Let's drink to your grandfather's memory. He was a great man. He will be missed by many." She raised her glass and said, "May his memory be eternal."

We drank and then we drank some more. Then we

continued drinking until it was way past dark and the restaurant empty. Katrina motioned for us to sit when we tried to get up. "We just started," she said with a big roar.

"No, I have to get home." I slurred my words. It took a lot to get me drunk. I think I'd gotten there. Erik smiled, holding me up as I slumped. "You're too drunk to drive."

"My grandfather's car."

"It's fine. We'll pull it around the back for you. You catch a cab and head home," Katrina said.

We walked out of the tearoom into the cold Chicago wind rising from the lake, whipping around us. I could see Erik didn't feel a thing. Flakes of lake-effect snow blew into the night, freezing on my eyelids. My white-blond hair turned pure white. The snow melted off the heat radiating from Erik's body. What kind of Norse God was this man? I stumbled, walking to the curb to hail a cab. He grabbed me and pulled me back. I grew dizzy. He hailed a cab and placed me gently inside, sitting next to me. I managed to tell the driver the address, and then I passed out.

Chapter Sixteen

When I woke the next morning, my head ached. Pure vodka never gives me a headache, but those flavored ones with the infusions… Hunter lay next to me, Gem on my feet. I sat up; my head felt worse. Erik walked into the bedroom, carrying a glass of water and a bottle of Tylenol. I took both gladly. He leaned against the doorjamb. "What time is it?" I asked.

"It's nearly one o'clock."

I looked at the sun peeking in through the curtains.

"One o'clock in the afternoon," he repeated.

"Oh," I said. I glanced under the covers. I pulled the sheet up around me when I realized I was naked. "Hey, what happened to my clothes?"

"You were sick when we got here and threw up a couple of times. I had to wash you down. I put you in the shower. You don't remember that? I couldn't find any clean clothes for you." Erik glanced down at the floor.

My face turned red. Hunter jumped up and gave Erik a lick. Erik ruffled his fur. I've never seen Hunter take to anyone, especially a man. He was very cautious with Erik at first, but Erik had won his trust. "Let me find some clothes, and I'll make us some breakfast," I said, pulling the sheet closer around me. When Erik nodded in agreement but didn't move, I added, "Well, get out. I've got to get dressed."

"Oh." He left the room, closing the door behind him.

I searched through my grandfather's dresser drawers and found his red plaid flannel short-sleeve shirt. I threw it on. I went into the bathroom and splashed water on my face, put a little Crest on my fingertip, and brushed my teeth. I pulled my hair back in a ponytail. I pulled the left side of the shirt down off my shoulder to see the scar on my upper arm from the gunshot. It was healing nicely. The scars from my shoulder surgery were still pink. Those would never look much better. I looked in the mirror. I was twenty-six years old, and life had beaten me up pretty good. I went down the stairs into the kitchen. Erik had the old percolator going with fresh coffee. I checked the fridge; nothing in there. Or what *was* there had gone bad. I checked the cabinets and found some instant oatmeal. I mixed it with hot water, threw in some brown sugar and butter and found a box of raisins and filled two bowls. I sat down across from Erik.

"You look very nice," he said.

"You know the dresser was full of shirts. I could have worn one of those last night."

Erik smiled and sipped his coffee.

I took the necklace off and placed it in the center of the table. "Whoever broke into our shop and killed my grandfather then tried to kill me was after this necklace. Why now?"

Erik didn't answer. He had no answer.

"This is all a fairy tale. The Romanovs' buried treasure," I continued.

"Even if *we* don't believe it, someone does. I think we need to figure this out," Erik said.

I picked the necklace up and ran it through my fingers. "*The dead shall live.* What the hell does that mean?"

"*The dead shall live* must be a reference to the

seven buried coffins. The treasure was hidden with the hope that the Romanovs would escape their fate," Erik said.

"Or perhaps the Grand Duke knew they wouldn't be saved, but a piece of them would live on through their treasure," I said. "And, if we believe the necklace, those coffins are buried somewhere in the region of Ekaterinburg. Why leave such a cryptic message?" I asked.

"He was planning to run away with her. He must have wanted to leave a clue in case something happened to him. She must have known how to decipher it."

"What do we do now?" I finished my coffee. My head was clearing up.

"I calculated the directions and the longitude and latitude is in the center of Ekaterinburg. After the revolution, it became the administrative center of the area. It'd be a good place to start our search. They should have a history of the pre- and post-revolution."

"Ekaterinburg? That's where the Romanovs were killed," I said, recalling my Russian history.

"It would seem to be an opportune place to hide imperial treasure if the Grand Duke was trying to help his cousin escape. Seven coffins full of jewels could bribe a lot of guards."

I picked up the alexandrite necklace again. "This necklace is the first half of the map, deciphering it is the second half. If he meant this for his lover, he must have given her the key to the puzzle. I think we need to find out who she was. We should go see my father." We finished our coffee and headed to my father's shop.

My father was in the back of the shop, showing Kiri the proper way to assess stones, using a magnifying loupe and calipers. He had an array of uncut stones on the table in front of him. "Alex, Kiri's a natural. He has an amazing eye." My father was beaming.

"He knows his way around gems," I agreed. "Father, Erik and I wanted to talk to you." I noticed my father give Erik a stern nod before I continued. "We deciphered the inscription on the stones on the necklace. It was written in Morse code, directing us to the city of Ekaterinburg near the Ural Mountains. The rest of the message reads: *The dead shall live*."

My father laughed his deep belly laugh. "Alexandra, I know the fairy tales of the Grand Duke and the seven buried coffins. And that's all it is. A fairy tale."

"Someone killed grandfather for the necklace and its secret."

"You don't know that."

I pulled up my sleeve and showed the scar on my arm. "Someone tried to kill me in Vancouver for the necklace."

"Why didn't you tell me about this? What's wrong with you?" My father stood up and looked at my arm. Concern lines framed his forehead.

"I didn't want you to worry."

"I'm your father. It's my job to worry."

"This isn't going to stop until they get their hands on the necklace and me."

"What do you want to do, Alexandra?"

"Erik and I are going to fly to Ekaterinburg. We have to find out who the duke's lover was and if she knew the meaning of the phrase, *The dead shall live*. The necklace is a treasure map. We have to find out its secret."

"You're not going without me. If someone is after you, they'll have to go through me."

"What about Kiri?"

"It would be good for Kiri to see the family homeland," my father said.

"Family?"

"He's part of our family now."

Kiri sat smiling, dangling his foot off the chair. I turned to them and said, "Erik, Kiri, can you give my father and me a moment alone please?"

Erik grabbed Kiri's soccer ball and took him out to the alley.

"Father, you're building up Kiri's hopes here. We don't know how long he'll be with us. They might find a permanent family for him any day now. That transition will be more difficult for him the more attached he gets to you."

"What would be so wrong if he stayed with us? Why can't he be part of our family?"

"I can't take an eight-year-old around the world with me. I can't be responsible." I sat on the stool Kiri had vacated.

"He can stay with me. I have room upstairs."

"We don't have time to figure this out now. I contacted Carter. He's going to let us use his plane. It's at Midway. We're leaving at five."

"It's all settled then. Kiri and I are going with you." My father crossed his arms. I knew there was no point in arguing with him.

"Erik and I are going to Minna's apartment. We'll meet you at the airport."

I packed quickly, then dropped Gem at Katrina's apartment above the restaurant. I didn't have the heart to leave Hunter again. I had left him so often in the past few years. I didn't know how much longer he would be with me. It was time he saw the motherland.

We walked Hunter into Minna's building. Most

dogs in the buildings were lap or purse dogs. The residents were not used to one of Hunter's size. They stayed clear of him as we entered the lobby and went to the penthouse. "I've heard nothing back from the police. They're not considering Minna as anything other than a missing person. They have no leads to follow and are convinced that Minna took off on her own," I told Erik.

I opened the door with the key Minna had left me for emergencies. I considered this an emergency. Nothing had changed since I'd been here last. Erik walked around, touching the dead flowers. He knew Minna well enough to know that these flowers would have been unacceptable to her. Hunter sniffed the floors, emitting low growls. He was never a fan of Minna's, but he tolerated her because I loved her. That wasn't why he was growling. He was more intense than I'd ever seen him, clawing at blankets, growling at the corners of the room like there was a ghost we couldn't see.

Erik unscrewed one of the vent covers. He shook his head, confirming there were no listening devices. Then he spoke. "There's nothing here that would indicate where she's gone to except she couldn't have left the country without her passport." He looked at Minna's picture on the passport, which still sat on her bed. "Even if she did leave in a hurry, why wouldn't she have taken her jewelry?"

I went through her jewelry box, picking things up from the floor. "These are all nice pieces, everyday pieces. Things she would wear to go to the store or to tea. I've seen her in necklaces worth hundreds of thousands of dollars, rings worth the same. She wouldn't have bothered if she was in a hurry to take any of this."

"What about the Fabergé egg?" Erik asked,

glancing at the ornate green-and-gold treasure, which sat in its place of honor.

I picked it up and turned it over. The weight felt wrong. It was lighter than it should be. I took out my loupe and examined the rubies. "This is all glass and crystal. It's a reproduction. I never knew. Everything Minna has is the best, original, estate vintage pieces. That's why she left it."

"She didn't leave it. She was taken," Erik said. He pulled me over by the bed to Minna's trunk. There was a red stain on the bedspread under the suitcase.

"Is that blood?"

Erik nodded.

I pulled the duvet off. The stain soaked through to the mattress. "I never moved the trunk when I was here. I didn't see the blood."

"Now there's reason for the police to get involved."

I held back tears. I hadn't wanted to admit it to myself. The thought had crept into my head many times. Minna with the shadow man, the man who killed my grandfather, the man who tried to kill me, but the truth was before my eyes. Blood doesn't lie. I sat on the edge of the bed and let everything go. My grandfather... Minna. I hadn't cried since my mother had died when I was five. Her death wasn't sudden. No, it was much worse. She lingered between worlds for a year—in and out of the hospital, in and out of chemo until she was a young old frail woman at twenty-eight. That's when my father started looking at me as his son, wanting to toughen me up to protect me from her fate, to protect me from the world and anything in it that could take me from him like his wife was taken. That's when I stopped crying. Now I sat here in front of a man I hardly knew, with all my emotions pouring out. Erik sat on the edge of the bed next to me and put his arm around me. I buried my face in his chest. I didn't care anymore. It was the sweet release of letting to. I held myself in check for so long I had forgotten how to be vulnerable. I forgot how to let people into my life, into my heart.

My sadness turned to anger. I glanced up at Erik. Minna had meant just as much to him. I could see the pain in his eyes. I kissed his cheeks. I kissed his lips. We clung to each other.

Erik whispered, "*Hamndaktion*. We will have our revenge."

I straddled his lap and put my arms around his neck. This time when I kissed him, it was more than a thank-you, more than a simple pleasure. I cared about this man. My phone vibrated in my pocket. I stopped kissing him, pulled out my phone. "Erik, my father's at the airport. We have to go." I stood up, motioned for Hunter. He ran to my side. I knelt down and whispered, "*Hamndaktion*. That's Swedish for we'll have our revenge, Hunter. In our language, its '*zhazhda mesti.*' You and I will taste blood, my old friend."

Chapter Seventeen

A soft snow fell on the ground as we reached Midway. My father and Kiri were already on board the jet. Kiri was showing my father how to work the satellite TV, flipping through the channels until he found a soccer match. Manchester United was playing Germany. Kiri squealed with excitement and jumped in my father's lap.

The flight attendant carried a tray, a silver bucket full of candy bars, a basket of chips. Kiri looked stunned. I could hear him ask my father, "Do we have money for that? How much is it?"

"No, Kiri, those are all free."

"Which one is mine?"

"Kiri, anyone you want. For this trip anyway."

Kiri took his time deciding, touching each candy bar. It was a big decision. He retrieved a $100,000 bar and sighed. "This is a lot of money. Can we afford this?"

My father laughed his deep laugh. "That's just the name of the candy bar. It's good that you ask first, but you may have it."

Kiri unwrapped the bar, took a bite, closing his eyes, savoring the chocolate and then returned to watching the game. My father motioned to the flight attendant who brought him bottled water. I sat down next to him, staring at the water. He gave me a surprised look. "What's troubling you?" Then he looked at the water. "I need to cut back on my vodka." My father nodded his head toward Kiri. "Not a good example for the boy."

Hunter walked up and down the aisle, not understanding the feeling of flight. I comforted him, rubbing his ear, nuzzling his nose. Kiri walked up to him and put his arms around him. They stood eye to eye. Hunter licked Kiri's face. Like with Erik, Hunter and Kiri had formed a friendship. It reassured me what a good person Kiri was.

Erik sat quietly staring out the window. He had not had a drink the whole flight. My father was eying Carter's selection of premium vodkas and playing with the inflight movie selection until he found *Rocky IV* where Rocky battles the much larger Russian. It always made my father laugh. He chose another bottle of sparkling water and sat down to watch the movie with Kiri, explaining the humor of a tiny American beating up a much larger Russian.

Hours later, we landed at the Ekaterinburg airport. Coming from Chicago, our blood was used to the ten degree cold. I put on my down coat and helped Kiri into his Columbia jacket. My father wore his suit jacket. He wanted to look good for when he stepped onto Russian soil. He refused to bring a jacket with him. We exited the plane and walked through customs. I held Hunter's leash. The official waved us through, giving Hunter an admiring glance. Carter's people had arranged for a Range Rover and a driver waiting for us outside the airport. We loaded up and headed to our hotel. The driver took us to the Hyatt Regency, another reservation handled by Carter's people.

"I will be here when you need me. Mr. Carter reserved me for your entire stay," the driver said, handing me a card with his number as we pulled up in front of the hotel.

"Thank you," I said, taking the card and putting it

in my pocket.

"I'll go check us in," Erik said, entering the lobby. I stayed outside to walk Hunter in front of the modern, high-rise hotel near the city square.

Hunter blended into the landscape. Gorbatov couldn't have painted a more perfect Russian wolfhound. His breed was as old as the cobblestone sidewalk that we walked, the only remaining remnants of the ancient city, now industrialized and a modern metropolis. His large chest heaved in and out, breathing the cool Russian air. His eyes sparkled and smiled up at me. I felt this was where he was meant to be. Something in his blood told him this is where he came from.

I went up to my hotel room and got ready. I opened my suitcase, which was filled with the tools I needed. A 9-millimeter Glock, my bench-made boot knife. I strapped on both and threw on a pair of jeans and a flannel shirt. I grabbed my North Face jacket and my backpack.

I met the rest of my group in the lobby. My father was showing Kiri some of the paintings that hung in the hotel's lobby. These were scenes depicting imperial Russia. In their center was a large oil frame painting of the Romanov family. Nicholas was in dress uniform, Alexandra in a jewel-encrusted gown just like in my dream. I shuddered for a moment. I listened as my father explained that this city was the place where the royal family had been held captive and finally executed.

"Kiri, in 1998, the Russian government held a state funeral for the Romanovs as a part of an apology for the slaying of their family. We should pay our respects at the Church on Blood," my father said.

Our guide, whom the hotel provided for us, met us

in the lobby. We followed him out onto the street as he led us toward the Church on Blood. "The church is built on the site where the Romanovs were murdered. It commemorates the Romanov sainthood," he told us in perfect English.

We could see the church's gold onion-shaped turrets as we walked toward it. We walked up the steps that led to the entrance. Outside were large black-and-white images of the Romanov family and statues of Nicholas and Alexandra. Inside, the church resembled a typical Russian orthodox structure built in the Byzantine style, gold-leaf tapestries hung on the walls near portraits of the family. We stood in the main church while our guide explained quietly that the altar stood on the site where the family had been executed. My father did the sign of the cross and said a prayer as we watched in silence.

We then walked next door to the museum that honored the imperial family.

Our guide explained how the church had been built on the site of the former Ipatiev house, a local merchant's house in Ekaterinburg. This was where the imperial family had been held captive. "The Soviets tore down the Ipatiev house in the 1970s. Later, the remains of the family were found by locals who kept their location secret for many years until Communism collapsed. In 1991, five of the bodies including the czar, czarina, and three of their daughters were exhumed. After DNA testing, they were laid to rest with state honors in St. Petersburg. The other two bodies were discovered in 2007. In August 2000, the Russian Orthodox Church announced the canonization of the family, and in October 2008, the Russian court ruled that the Romanovs were victims of political repression and rehabilitated them."

As the guide spoke, I walked over to a large framed photograph that was hanging on the sidewall. It was a picture of Czar Nicholas and Alexandra in the Ipatiev house, next to them was a general and a woman. The caption read General Yurokov and his wife, Catherine Yurokova. Though the photograph was grainy and deteriorated, there was no mistaking the necklace she was wearing. I ran my fingers along the stones of Catherine's necklace. Even in the photograph, I could see the despair in her eyes, the sadness for what was coming. I motioned for the guide to come over. "Who is this general in this photograph?"

"That's an interesting story. General Yurokov was a trusted confidante to Nicholas II. He fought next to him on the front lines in World War I. The general returned to Moscow while Nicholas stayed on the front lines. He disagreed with Alexandra's influence on the government. He felt she sympathized with the Germans because she was German. He also didn't approve of her relationship with Rasputin. This led him to join the Bolsheviks and fight against Nicholas. He was in charge when they were held captive here."

"What about his wife?"

"The story says she was a Romanov sympathizer and brought them food and made them as comfortable as she could. She played games with the younger children. She disappeared right before the family was assassinated. It was never clear what happened to her. The general became a powerful leader in the Soviet army and eventually became the ambassador to the United States in Washington."

"Do you know her maiden name?"

"No, I don't know much about her other than she went missing right about the time of the assassination. Many of the records aren't clear during the revolution. Many of the records were destroyed or lost. Pretty much everything in the museum is all that is left from that time. You can try the hall of records if you want to learn more."

"Can you tell me how to get to the hall of records?"

Kiri ran up to me. "Excuse me, excuse me, Alex. I'm hungry. Can we eat?"

"Sure, Kiri, let's gather everyone." I thanked our guide and followed Kiri outside where Erik and my father were waiting, smoking, my father holding Hunter's leash. I could tell my father had been quizzing Erik about our relationship. He'd apparently opened the minibar in his room because he was a bit drunk, angry, and getting angrier. Hunter circled around the two men, moaning. He pulled away from my father and ran up to Kiri. He lay down at his feet and growled. "Hunter, what's wrong?" I asked.

Hunter wouldn't leave Kiri's feet. The Borzoi was shaking. I'd never seen him shake before. My father grabbed Erik by the arm.

"Father what are you doing?"

"This guy says you spent the night at your grandfather's house. What were you doing there?" My father's face turned red, and his voice became a deep demanding bark.

"We got drunk with Katrina. He brought me home. I was too drunk to get home on my own. And my companions were at grandfather's. I can't leave them alone overnight."

"I don't like this guy. I don't trust him."

Before I could answer him, Hunter stood up and ran off into the street, barking wildly. "Hunter!" I screamed, running after him. I chased him for blocks. As I turned the corner of a small street of shops, I saw him at the end of a dead-end alley, barking up at a fire escape. "Hunter!" I yelled again. He wouldn't stop barking or circling the fire escape. I couldn't see what he was barking at. I'd never known him to act like this. And then the garbage cans rattled, and a feral cat climbed out, hissing, running past Hunter.

I grabbed Hunter's leash and walked him back to where we'd left the others. It appeared that my father had still not solved his argument with Erik.

"Alexandra, what's wrong with the dog?" my father asked.

"I don't know. You've had enough to drink. Let's get something to eat."

Our guide recommended a small restaurant near the hotel. We walked in the cold winter air. Kiri and I were bundled up in our down jackets, my father and Erik in their suit jackets. The hostess led us to a table in the back. They did not hesitate letting Hunter in. "What a beautiful dog!" the hostess said. "We don't see very many Borzoi anymore."

"Thank you," I said, holding Hunter's leash as she reached to pet him. He slipped back behind me. We sat at the table. Hunter lay at my feet. Erik and my father both reached for the chair next to me. Erik won and sat down. My father sat across from me.

"Vodka," he said as the waitress came over to take our order.

"Father, you need to eat something," I said.

"First we start with vodka."

I knew this was an argument that I wasn't going to win. The waitress brought over a bottle of vodka for the table and poured glasses for my father, Erik, and myself. Kiri sipped at his water. My father ordered several appetizers, including a cheese and vegetable tray. He followed that by ordering the traditional meat platter with several steaks and local sausages and lamb tongue. I added an order of french fries for

Kiri and baked mushrooms for the table.

As we ate the cheese and vegetables, I told my father and Erik about the picture of the general and his wife. "She was wearing the necklace." I brought up the image I'd taken of the picture on my iPhone.

"That's the necklace, Alexandra." My father agreed with me, downing another glass of vodka.

"Our guide said that no one knows what happened to her, that she was a Romanov sympathizer. We need to go to the hall of records and see what we can find out about Catherine Yurokova." I took my phone back and put it in my pocket.

"We'll go there first thing tomorrow morning."

As the waitress brought out plate after plate, Kiri's eyes grew larger and larger. He ate quickly as if he was afraid the food would disappear. "Kiri, slow down. You're going to upset your stomach," my father told him.

"I'll go with you in the morning," Erik said. His hand touched mine as he reached for another piece of rye toast. I shivered slightly at his touch, feeling that spark of electricity. I pulled my hand away and put it in my lap.

"No, I'll go with her," my father said. He glared at Erik as if trying to make out our relationship.

"I can go by myself."

"I'll go with you. I'm the only one here who speaks fluent Russian," my father commanded.

"Of course you'll go with me," I said. "Erik will stay with Hunter and Kiri."

"It's decided then."

We finished our meal, completing it with slices of cheesecake and chocolate truffle. Kiri's head bent over the table. "Let's get the boy back to the hotel," I said.

Erik reached over to Kiri to pick him up. My

father pushed him out of the way and picked the slight boy up. "I'll carry him."

We walked the few blocks back to the hotel. "I'll be right in," I said. "I'm going to stay out with Hunter for a few minutes."

Hunter sniffed the air, his tail curling up delicately. His broad chest breathed the cool air in and out. I pulled my down coat tighter around as I watched my father go into the hotel, still carrying Kiri. Erik stood next to me. "I can't leave you out here at night," he said.

"I can take care of myself," I said though I was thankful of his company. Hunter still seemed on alert as he had since he'd run off from us at the museum. We walked around the block. The early night sky was washed with stars, temperatures dropping down close to zero degrees. We could see the fog on our breath. We settled on a park bench overlooking the square.

"Your father doesn't like me."

"He needs to get to know you. He's very protective as you've seen," I said. "I'm all the family he has left. What about your family?"

"Both my parents died. I have a sister who lives in Stockholm. She's married with two children," Erik said. "I stop to see them a few times a year around Christmas and her birthday. I also have a brother who lives in Chicago. I don't see him very much anymore."

"You've never been married?"

"No, I've never been married. I travel too much. Not too many women want to stay home alone, months at a time. It's not a good life for a wife," Erik said.

I understood. I led the same life, never in one place for very long, always traveling, on to the next find. Neither one of us had mentioned Minna since we'd left her apartment. "I'm worried about Minna. I'm afraid she's dead."

"I don't know about that. Minna can handle herself."

"All that blood. How could she survive that?"

"How much do you know about Minna?"

"She's always been around, friend of the family. My grandfather and grandmother met her in the late 1960s. She was always part of the Chicago Russian community. We've always been close. She's watched out for me and taught me a lot about gem hunting. How about you?"

"I left the Swedish air force and was doing some mercenary work. Minna was buying black market stones that were smuggled out of Afghanistan. She hired me to fly her out of Tijkastin when the rebels took the city. My team was killed, and I was badly wounded. Minna traded the stones for my life and brought me to safety. I owe my life to her. I'm not going to rest until I find her."

"Why are you telling me all this now?"

"Because I'm in this till the end. I owe Minna."

I let the information soak in. I couldn't grasp what he was saying. This was the sweet though hard-edged woman I'd known since I was a little girl. I knew her more as mentor, a confidant. She came to my ballet recitals, my high school graduation. She was always around when there were family events—happy or tragic. For whatever reasons, she kept her past private. I understood. That was the Russian way. My father and grandfather were the same. I think that's what keeps me from letting people into my life.

Here I sit next to the most handsome, interesting man I've ever met. Someone whom I trusted, someone whom I wanted, and I still couldn't bring myself to let him in. Hunter rubbed his head against

my leg. I put my arms around him and rubbed his soft
fur.

Chapter Eighteen

Erik had taken Kiri and Hunter to the park, while my father and I headed to the hall of records, a three-story building in the heart of the city. My father spoke with the woman at the reception desk, who led us to the section of the building that held marriage licenses. Rows of books lined the metal shelves. "You said you were looking for pre-Soviet records. Those are in the original books. Do you know what year?" the receptionist asked.

"Nyet." My father shook his head.

"The woman we're looking for was in her early twenties in 1917, so we could start with 1910 or 1911," I said.

The woman pulled out a large red bound book and put it on the desk. "This is 1910 if you want to start here. These aren't the actual marriage licenses. It's just the ledger."

For the next hour, my father and I each sifted through the books, looking for General Yurokov. By book seven, we found his name. "Alexandra, look." My father pointed to the names on the page.

"General Boris Yurokov and Catherine Ruskova," I read over his shoulder. Father, that's her." I wrote down the name and returned the books to the shelves. We walked over to the department of health to find death certificates for Ekaterinburg. This time we were certain of the year. There were no death certificates issued for either Catherine Ruskova or Yurokova; however, in 1918 there were several death certificates issued with the name Ruskova—perhaps relatives of Catherine. From the binder, I wrote down all the names and the last known addresses.

None of the addresses were current. None of the names matched up with Catherine's. The last address on the list led us to a small farm on the outskirts of town. Not really a farm—it wasn't more than a few acres of untilled rocky soil and a small frame farmhouse. We knocked on the door. An old woman answered, clutching a wooden cane. "Yes, may I help you?" she asked in Russian.

My father spoke. I could understand most of what he was saying, but I couldn't speak or comprehend as quickly as he could. The last part I understood; the old woman asked us in. The inside of the farmhouse was more dilapidated than the outside. Its only furnishings were a primitive wood table, a wood-burning stove, a small cot under the window, and a fire burning brightly. Standing out of place in the corner was a beautiful, hand-carved walnut armoire. She sat us at the small table and brought us tea.

I pulled out my iPhone. "Catherine, do you know this woman?" I showed her the picture I'd taken of the general's wife.

She motioned for me to wait and retrieved a pair of glasses. "My eyes aren't so good," she said in broken English, taking my phone from me. She looked carefully at the photo again, moving the phone closer and then farther away from her, trying to focus. "Where did you get this photograph?"

"It's hanging in the museum at the Church on Blood."

"I've never been there. I don't go into town much." She left again and walked over to the armoire. It was a beautiful hand-carved piece that stood out from the rest of the furnishings. She opened it, and I saw an ornate gold gilt Fabergé egg that appeared to be an exact match of Minna's. She brought over a silver-framed photograph. It was a wedding picture of General Yurokov and his wife Catherine. "This is all I have left of my great-aunt's. I was named after her." She ran her finger along Catherine's long brown hair as she smiled a toothless grin. Then she frowned. "The Soviets took everything else of hers. That's why I never go into town."

I got up and looked at the egg. It was exactly like Minna's. "May I take a closer look?"

"Yes. I've hidden it all these years. It was against the law to hold imperial treasure."

I picked it up and held it in my hand. Unlike Minna's, this one had weight. I took my loupe out and examined the stones; they were real. This was a real imperial treasure.

"Why you asking about my great-aunt?"

"My great-grandfather was a friend of hers." I pulled the cowl neck of my sweater down to show the necklace. "This belonged to your great-aunt. My great-grandfather made it for her."

The old woman put her glasses on the tip of her nose and looked closely at it, touching the stones. "May I hold it?"

I handed her the necklace. She walked over to the fire and held it in front of the flames. "The dead shall live."

"How did you know how to read the necklace?"

She took the Fabergé egg from my hand and twisted it along its perforation in the middle. She held it up for me to see. Along the top and the bottom of the separated egg etched in gold were several lines of Morse code that circled the egg. My father looked closely. She turned the top part of the Fabergé egg so the Morse code letter *d* lined up with the one and only alexandrite stone—the centerpiece of the egg. Each time she turned the egg, lining up the corresponding letters with the alexandrite, the four connecting lines deciphered the code. She read the message out loud, "d-e-a-d s-h-a-l-l l-i-v-e in the house of salt."

I typed into my phone as she read. "She's talking about the salt mines under the city, the Ipatiev house sits on top of them," I said, gazing at my father.

"Dead shall live," my father said. "The coffins of the Romanovs."

The old woman placed the Fabergé egg back into the cabinet, running her finger along it. She placed the photo next to it and then closed the doors. "The Soviets killed most of my relatives because they were sympathizers of the Romanovs. My mother passed this Fabergé egg down to me and showed me how to read the message but I don't know what it means."

"What happened to your aunt?"

The old woman shook her head. "We don't know; no one knows. My mother said there were no official records. There was no funeral, but we knew my great-aunt's husband, the general, murdered her. He was a very jealous man and much older than her. My mother also told me about the necklace that you're wearing and that it was not a gift from her husband. The necklace is useless without the egg, and the egg without the necklace. My aunt's lover wanted to make sure they would share the treasure together."

"Thank you, Catherine; thank you so much. This is a part of my family history that has been missing for a long time also," I said. As our hands touched, a spark of electricity surged between us.

The old woman gave me a look of recognition. "You have the gift," she said. "Wait!" She reached back into the cabinet and returned carrying something. She put it in my hand, closing my fingers around hers. It was the egg.

"I can't take this," I said, handing it back toward her.

"You must," she insisted. "You know what to do with it."

I glanced at her and then at my father. He nodded. This generosity was the Russian way. To argue would be impolite. "Thank you," I said, hugging her.

She smiled her toothless grin. We stepped back into the cold and climbed into the Range Rover. My father drove back to town.

"Alexandra, the salt mines are closed. They've been closed for many years. You need special permission even to go into the areas that are safe. The other areas are filled with poisonous gas and landslides. I don't think this is a good idea."

"Whoever killed grandfather killed him for whatever's down in those salt mines," I said. "He's not going to stop until he finds the treasure, and I want to be there when he does."

My father couldn't help but smile. "I understand, Malenkaya. I want to hold that man's throat in my hands too."

We reached the hotel where Kiri, Erik, and Hunter were waiting. Kiri was enjoying a hot chocolate. Hunter begged for marshmallows and Kiri was obliging him. When Kiri saw us walk into the marble entry, he flew up to us, Hunter on his heels, first hugging my father and then me.

My father petted his head and said, "Hello, Malenkaya."

We joined Erik in front of the fire, sitting on the overstuffed leather chairs and couches. My father motioned over for the concierge. "Bring pastries and coffee."

I began to tell Erik the story of the old woman. His

eyes sparkled as I spoke. I could see he had the same blood lust to avenge Minna.

My father interrupted. "The mines are off-limits. There's not enough time to get special permission. According to what we understand from the coordinates from the necklace, whatever it is we're to find is buried six hundred fifty feet under the city. It's a labyrinth full of layers of mineral carnallite with magnesium chloride that causes poisonous gas leaks and landslides. It's easy to get lost. Many of the passageways look exactly the same with psychedelic swirling colors of yellow, brown, and blue. Almost hypnotizing. Methane, hydrogen sulfide and carbon dioxide are all down there."

"But the reward is worth the risk," I said. "What if it's the hiding place of the seven coffins of the imperial family? It would be worth billions of dollars in precious jewelry and loose gems."

"It's not ours."

"It's not ours, but I won't let it be taken by the man who took grandfather. I'm gathering gear. I'm leaving for the mines first thing in the morning."

"I want to go too," Kiri said

"It's too dangerous. You can stay here with my father—Pappa."

"Alex, you're not going down there without me," my father said.

"I'm going too," Erik said.

I looked around at my friends and family. We were all in this together. Kiri was no safer above ground than below with whomever was after the necklace. Whatever we found we'd find together.

Chapter Nineteen

I checked my backpack, flashlights, rope, water, emergency kit and power bars. I slipped my knife into my boot and put my 9-millimeter Glock in the back of my jeans. I pulled my sweater over it to conceal it. I met everyone in the lobby. We climbed in the Range Rover and headed to the southeast corner of the town where the street ended and the gravel began.

I drove the SUV as far back into the woods as we could, and then we jumped out. Without permits, we wouldn't be able to enter the mine by the main entrance. Erik was able to find a topographical map of the town along with a thermal map of the mine underneath it. As we walked through the dense spruce trees, it began to snow. Hunter pranced in the new falling snow, snapping at the snowflakes. Kiri did the same. At first the large flakes clung to my eyelids and then turned into heavy wet snow. Not more than a mile off the road, we reached the abandoned entrance. It had been boarded over a long time ago, the spruce trees hiding it from view.

Erik picked up a large branch and pried off the rotting board. I shined a light inside. I could immediately smell the salt and the stale air. I took out my small methane gas monitor. Checking for gas was something I was used to doing. There were no signs of methane or any other poisonous gas. We'd been unable to acquire masks without raising suspicion. It was a risk we were willing to take.

We entered the mine. As I shone my light on the walls, it was like my father said—psychedelic swirls from strip-mining salt. It was as though someone had painted a Peter Max mural. The walkway into the mine slowly descended, taking us farther into the darkness. Particles of salt danced in the air, lofting up in the wake of our steps. I glanced down at Kiri, who was smiling. He was as familiar with mines as I was. He'd spent his young life in Cambodia looking for any scraps of red, blue, and purple. He touched the walls. I explained that it was a natural phenomenon, the scraping of the mineral carnallite, the source of magnesium used for crop fertilizers.

The tunnels ran every direction for miles. I counted steps according to the direction from the necklace. In 1917, there was no GPS, there was no Google Earth—just a man hiding treasure under a city, counting his steps, numbering his turns, looking for the perfect spot to hide the last remnants of the imperial way of life. Eventually the mine floor gave way to an open cavern with a small catwalk along the edge that the miners had used to navigate the mine. The small wooden railing was rotten and falling apart. I reached behind me and held Kiri up against the wall as we walked to make sure he didn't misstep. After we crossed it, we saw three tunnels. I took out my methane meter. The meter bounced slightly.

Erik, who'd taken the lead, turned to me. "Which tunnel?"

I opened my iPhone to read the notes that I had deciphered using the egg. We'd followed the map and from what I could calculate we were under the Church on Blood, the site of the Ipatiev house. The message had not said which tunnel to take from this point. We'd entered the farthest southeast entrance of the mine, followed the catwalk, and reached the three tunnels. But the decipher text wasn't clear. It read *enter the tunnel a thousand feet.*

"Erik, it doesn't say which tunnel."

"I'll take the one on the left," Erik said. "Kiri and Peter can take the middle. Alex, take the right."

We split up, Hunter following me into the cavern. I counted out a thousand steps as I walked. At least that's what I thought the code required. The tunnel narrowed to the point where I had to hunch over. I thought of India. My shoulder ached. Then finally I was on my hands and knees, Hunter scooting behind me. My breathing was labored. I took out my meter. Now the meter was steady, nearing the redline, the line I didn't dare cross. I could hear Hunter panting heavily behind me. We continued on. This part of the mine had caved in. There was barely enough room for me to squeeze through. Hunter whimpered. I stopped to catch my breath, which was harder and harder to do. Once again, I thought back to my experience in India. I regretted following that dangerous crevice into the darkness, and then I thought about the reward—the alexandrite. I thought about my grandfather, about Minna, and I crawled forward.

I pushed away small boulders, gravel and piles of salt. The tiny crevice opened up into a large room. I turned around, cleared the way for Hunter who pulled himself through. I checked my meter—the needle brushing up against the redline. This was the last part of the map. I had reached it. I looked around the walls. They were different than the rest of the mine— no psychedelic swirls, very little magnesium, not a very good source of salt. The perfect place to bury a treasure. A part of the mine where no one would ever venture. I unfolded the small shovel out of my backpack and started digging. I dug for what seemed like hours, checking my meter. Hunter dug for a while and then lay down. I could hear voices from behind me. I shone my light back down the thousand feet of corridor I'd crawled through, signaling for Erik. Even Erik struggled, squeezing through the hole, pushing away the loose rocks with Kiri and my father behind him.

"Nothing. Nothing in the other tunnels. They were all dead ends. They'd been mined out and shut down," Erik said.

"This room is different than the rest of the mines," I said.

Erik took his shovel out of his backpack and started digging. My father joined him. Hunter and Kiri walked along the edge of the large cavern. Wall to wall, it had to be at least three hundred feet. It would take us more time than we had to dig up the floor. Nearly two feet down and still no signs of a coffin or treasure. I checked my watch. We'd been in the cave nearly eight hours. Even with the methane levels under the red, I didn't want us breathing this air much longer.

Kiri sat watching, petting Hunter, picking up stones from the floor, shining his flashlight on them as though he'd find a ruby or sapphire. There'd be no such luck. No jewels under this mountain. He walked along the edges anyway. Picking up stones, shining his light. Then I heard him yell, "Miss Alex! Miss Alex, come, come!" Thinking he was hurt, I ran to the edge of the cavern. Kiri turned and smiled. He held up his little hand and shone a light through a chunk of rock. I peered at it closely. It was a polished alexandrite. "Like your necklace. Like your necklace!"

"Yes, very good, Kiri. Where'd you find it?"

He pointed to the far southeast corner wall. I took

his hand and reached along the wall, scraping my fingernails into the soft mineral-rich silt. It crumbled easily. I kept digging. I grabbed my shovel, digging deeper and deeper. Nearly five feet in, I struck the shovel hard and heard a clank. I hit it again. Another clank. Erik and my father turned at the noise. They ran over with their shovels to help me clear it away. They shone their lights in, and we all saw a piece of mahogany. I brushed away the remaining dirt and saw a brass handle. We continued to dig. The entire southeast wall of the cavern started to crumble. I grabbed Kiri and ran to the opposite wall. As the walls of the cave crumbled, I could hear the rest of the cave start to creak as dust rained from the ceiling. The seven coffins appeared through the dust, lying in the rubble. Erik and my father picked off the rocks on top of the coffins, pushing their shovels under the lids, trying to pry them open.

I checked my methane meter. It had reached the redline. "Kiri, get out now!"

"But Miss Alex, I want to see."

"Get out now and take Hunter with you," I said again, pushing the boy in the direction of the exit. He didn't move.

"Father." I showed my father my meter.

"Kiri, now!" He grabbed the small boy, lifting him off the ground. The two of them crawled out of the cavern. I could hear their footsteps as my father took them to fresh air.

Erik stared at me. "We have to go."

"I have to see what's inside."

Erik took his shovel and jammed it into the first coffin lid, trying to pry it open. "Alex, we have to go!"

I checked my meter. The needle was on the far edge of the thin redline. I took my shovel, stuck it in next to Erik's under the lid. Together we popped open the coffin. It was empty. Each coffin was the same. I checked my meter. Now the needle was past the redline. I didn't tell Erik. I had to see inside the last coffin. I stuck my shovel under the lid and popped it open. Inside was not the lost treasure of the Romanov dynasty. What lay in the coffin was something much more precious to the man who'd buried it here. It was a gilded silver-framed photo of Catherine Yurokova. I grabbed the photo. Erik and I crawled out of the cavern. My lungs were on fire, my shoulder ached, my head was dizzy. As we walked along the catwalk, the room swirled. I lost my gyroscope once again. I teetered over the edge and felt myself falling down into the dark hole beneath. And then I felt a hand grabbing me by the arm and pulling me up. Erik threw me over his shoulder. Behind us we heard the roar of the mine closing in. Even with his flashlight shining ahead, the mine was dark with dust. We both coughed. I lay over Erik's strong shoulder, putting the sleeve of my sweater over my mouth and nose trying to inhale as little of the salt and dirt as I could. I felt myself passing out.

Chapter Twenty

I opened my eyes. I could feel the wet snow under me. I closed my eyes and opened them again. My father and Erik sat cross-legged across from me on the ground, their hands tied behind their backs. I closed my eyes again. This time when I opened them, a strange face bent down, staring into my eyes. I tried to speak, but I was too weak. I didn't see Kiri or Hunter. The strange face shook me, grabbing my backpack, emptying it, staring at the photograph of Catherine. Then I felt his backhand cross my jaw. I saw stars and blacked out.

When I came to, my hands were tied behind me. I was sitting between Erik and my father. There was a fire. The strange face had built a fire. In front of all of us he sat on a stump throwing his knife into the ground and picking it up repeatedly looking down at the ground. When he looked up through the glow of the fire, I could see his face clearly for the first time. My head ached and my eyes were blurry. It wasn't the face I recognized but the shape. As he stood up, silhouetted by the fire's glow, it was the shadow man I'd seen at my grandfather's funeral. I could feel my knife in my boot. I wiggled trying to raise my leg far enough to reach it, but I couldn't.

Erik and my father sat quietly, watching. My father turned to me. I saw the deep cuts on his face still bleeding. His left eye was swollen and closed. I could see the blood stains in the snow around Erik, but I couldn't see any wounds. The shadow man walked over and crouched down in front of me. He took his hunting knife and rubbed the flat edge of it along one of my cheeks, then the other and then down my throat. Both my father and Erik strained at their bindings. Then he cut the necklace off my neck. He held it up to the fire, staring at the stones. He spoke in Russian. "You know all the trouble you've put me through for this necklace, and what do I have to show for it? All the coffins are empty."

"Who are you?" I asked.

He laughed. "Who am I? I'm the last face you're going to see."

"If you kill us, you'll never find what you're looking for."

He crouched down in front of me. This time he took the sharp edge of the blade and gently ran it down my throat down to my chest. A thin trickle of blood followed behind it. Erik leaped up, pushing him down. My father struggled to get up, but he was too weak. The shadow man stabbed Erik in the thigh. Erik fell to the ground. "If you kill him, I won't tell you," I yelled in Russian.

The shadow man sat cross-legged in front of me, wiping the blood off his knife onto the snow. "Talk."

"The Grand Duke buried the seven coffins with Romanov treasure in this mine. That we know. He wouldn't have buried them empty. The necklace was a message to his love, Catherine Yurokova. She was helping the Romanov family, relaying messages between Czar Nicholas and the Grand Duke. The Grand Duke had given her a Fabergé egg that was the decoder for the messages he used to pass to the czar. The last message he sent her was encrypted on that necklace. It was the location of the treasure in case anything happened to him. He wanted her to be safe, to be free of her husband. When the duke learned that

Catherine had been murdered, he moved the treasure and left that photograph as a way for anyone who found it to know how much he loved her and how they would never get their hands on the imperial treasure."

The shadow man smiled. "It's a very nice fairy tale. How will that help me?"

"I know where the Fabergé decoder egg is. It's worth millions."

The shadow man sat back down on the other side of the fire, took out a flask. He took a long drink and pondered what I'd told him. I could hear wolves howling in the distance. I could feel their eyes hunting us. I'd much rather deal with them than this man who sat across from me. He took another drink from his flask.

I whispered to my father. "Is Kiri alive?"

The crackle of the fire hid our voices. "When we came out of the mine, I saw this man waiting for us. I sent Kiri and Hunter off into the woods to hide. Before I could stop him, he hit Erik in the head with his rifle and then sliced me with his knife."

I listened to the wolves howl again. Hunter I knew would protect Kiri with his life, but he was old and there was only so much he could do. Erik righted himself on the ground, the blood gushing out of his leg. He wouldn't last much longer. I heard the bushes behind me rustling. If it were wolves, I'd rather die by their hand than the man who'd killed my grandfather. The shadow man walked back over and sat next to me, stroking my long hair. He whispered, "After I kill them, *we'll* have a little fun. Then you'll tell me where to find the egg and then I may or may not kill you. It'll be your choice how quickly you die."

As he stroked my hair, a small figure came rushing

out of the darkness. Kiri kicked with his carbon steel foot into the side of the shadow man's head. His eyes burst wide open, blood gushing from the new wound. Hunter leaped from the bushes, landing on top of him, tearing at his face and his throat.

"Kiri!" I yelled. "My boot!" He reached in, retrieved my knife, and cut me free. And then he did the same for my father and Erik. I ran over to my father.

"I'm fine. I'm fine. Take care of Erik."

I cut a piece of my sweater and made a tourniquet, tying it just above his knife wound. I put another piece on his wound. "Keep pressure on this." I turned to pull Hunter off the shadow man. There was no hurry. His throat and face had been torn to shreds. He lay lifeless, the crimson red soaking into the fresh white snow. Hunter looked up. His sweet white face full of blood, his broad chest heaving, his heart pounding. Wolves howled out from the darkness. Hunter howled back.

I hugged Kiri. "You did good. You did so good." I kissed him and hugged him again. "Are you okay?"

"I'm fine, Miss Alex. I'm fine. Hunter protected me. He chased away the wolves."

I went through the shadow man's pockets and found his phone. Photographs of my apartment, the store, Minna's penthouse, my grandfather's house, Erik and me standing on the river walk in Vancouver. I opened the recording app on his phone. We listened. It was the day before we'd left for Russia. The day we sat talking about flying to Ekaterinburg. Every step of the way the shadow man was behind us, always watching, always knowing what we would do next.

My father checked his wallet and said, "No passport, no ID."

"We have to get Erik to a hospital. He's lost a lot of blood," I said.

My father draped Erik over his shoulder and half walked him out of the woods back to the Range Rover. I drove through the snowfall, which had turned into a blizzard. I drove quickly on the icy roads, sliding left to right around curves.

Chapter Twenty-one

We sat in the family waiting room in the hospital emergency department. My father's wounds had been cleaned and stitched up. Hunter lay on the floor beside us next to the bench. The doctor had tested us all for methane poisoning and declared us fine. He'd told us we couldn't leave until we talked to the authorities. So now we were waiting for the police. We'd broken several international laws. With luck, the wolves would hide the shadow man for us.

My father contacted family, hoping someone could reach an attorney. I didn't have much hope for that happening. We were on our own. "Dad, I'm so sorry I dragged you into all this," I said. "All for nothing."

"It wasn't for nothing. I got to watch the man who killed my father die in front of me."

As we spoke, Kiri tugged on my sweater. "Just a minute, just a minute. I'm talking," I told him before turning back to my father. "But the imperial treasure is gone. It'll never be found." Kiri continued to tug on my sweater. I turned this time, a bit annoyed. "Kiri, it's impolite to interrupt when someone is speaking."

"Miss Alex, I have to show you."

The emergency room physician came out into the hallway and spoke to my father in Russian. "Erik will be fine. He lost a lot of blood. None of the wounds are fatal, but he won't be able to leave for a couple of days." My father translated.

"Can I see him?" I asked the doctor.

"He's waking up. You can go in." I ran into the recovery room. Erik's eyes were opened slightly. He smiled. "Quite an adventure we've had, Alex." He grabbed my hand.

"We'll have more."

"Can I tell you something?" he asked. He motioned for me to come closer. He grabbed the front of my sweater and pulled me down and kissed me. His heart monitor beeped quicker, and then he fell back asleep.

My father walked in the room and put his arm around me. "He's not a bad fellow."

We went back to the hallway. "Miss Alex, Miss Alex, I have to show you."

I knelt down in front of Kiri. "What is it, Kiri? What do you have to show me?"

"I found the alexandrite. It shouldn't have been in that cave."

"Yes, there's no alexandrite in this area. I think it was a mark left by the man who buried the coffins. Do you know the story of Hansel and Gretel leaving bread crumbs behind?" Then I realized Kiri couldn't fathom a story where children threw food away.

He shook his head no. "I found this when you were opening the coffins. The man who put them there must have dropped it." Kiri reached in his pocket and pulled out a diamond the size of his fist. My father and I stared. I took out my loupe. Its brilliance radiated, reflecting light in the way that only diamonds do.

"It has to be at least a hundred carats, flawless," my father said.

"It was one of Alexandra's favorite stones. I read about this in one of my histories of the world's jewels books," I said.

"That has to be worth over twenty million," my father said.

"What do we do with it?" I held it up to the light, watching the reflection of color. Its brilliance was unparalleled. I wrapped it in my scarf and placed it in my backpack next to the Fabergé egg. I gave Kiri a hug.

Kiri beamed. As I hugged Kiri, I could see over his shoulder several uniformed Russian police officers walking toward us. At the front of them was a man wearing a suit. He appeared to be their commander. He flashed his badge at my father. "Peter Kustodia, Alexandra Kustodia." He looked Kiri over and didn't acknowledge him. He did smile at Hunter, who growled. "The hospital administrator told me you were in the salt mines. What were you doing there?"

"We're gemologists from the United States. We have family in Russia. We heard about the salt mines. We always wanted to see them."

"You know there's proper protocol, permits, permissions that need to be given. The mines are very dangerous."

"My apologies, Captain; we're visitors to your country. We didn't realize we needed permission," I said.

"Let me see your passports."

I handed them over to him.

He checked both our passports. "Private plane. I see you're flying on a private plane. What about the man inside?" He nodded to Erik's room.

I handed him Erik's passport. He opened it and stared at Erik's picture. "We may have some questions for this man," the Captain said.

"The doctor said he won't be able to travel for a while."

The captain knelt down and gave Kiri a once-over and then looked at my father and me. "You have some very important friends, don't you? You're all free to go. It'd be best if you leave immediately."

I went in to say goodbye to Erik. "Are you sure you don't want me to stay?" I asked.

He tried to sit up. "No, go with your father and Kiri. They need you. I have to get to Thailand. Time to get back to work."

I turned to the door.

"Wait!" Erik said.

I looked back at him, then moved to his bedside.

He held up his hand and struggled to pull off the copper band around his right ring finger.

"This is for you," he said, dropping it in my hand.

"What is it?"

"It's a Viking ring. I found it by my house when I was little. It's twelve hundred years old. It hasn't been off my finger since I was twelve."

I took the ring. "How can I?"

"Take the ring." His hand closed around mine. "You hang onto it until I see you again." The morphine drip dropped another drip, and Erik was out again.

I stood for a minute looking at the Viking ring and then at the Viking who'd given it to me. I laid my ear down next to his chest to hear his heart beating. I wanted to hear it next to mine so many times but never had the courage to take a chance. I felt like a coward. Fearless about many things except letting myself love—that was something I couldn't do. With Erik, the reward would be worth the risk.

Chapter Twenty-two

Almost a day later, we landed at Midway Airport. We were greeted by Tom Carter and his entourage. Cameras clicked as Carter picked up Kiri and waved. When they stopped clicking, he put Kiri down. He patted him on the head. "Good trip?" he asked me, noticing my father's stitches and bruised face.

"Overall, a very good trip. Thank you for the plane. We appreciate it. I don't know how to thank you."

"Well, there is one thing. My girlfriend—you haven't met her yet—is giving me a bit of an attitude about my old girlfriend's necklace. She wants a stone she's read about. It's called Hiddenite. She wants it to be an engagement ring. We'll see about that. You think you could find that for me?" He flashed his twenty-million-dollar smile at me.

I smiled back. "We can make that happen."

"Great. I'll have my people call you to arrange it."

"Wait, you're coming too?"

"Of course."

"We'll talk about it."

"I have a car waiting for you to take you home."

I started walking away and then turned back to Carter. "Thank you for contacting the Russian police and arranging for our release."

He gave me a confused look. "What are you talking about? Release from what?"

"You didn't contact the authorities?"

"No. I don't know what you're talking about."

"Thank you for the plane."

Hunter jumped into the limousine first and then I followed him in, sliding over to make room for my father and Kiri. When Kiri got in, Hunter put his head on Kiri's lap. Kiri gently petted the dog's back. After ten minutes of driving, both dog and boy were sound asleep. My father reached for the liquor bar in the limousine. He poured himself a glass of Stoli. "I like the way this Tom Carter travels," he said, raising his glass to me and downing it. "Alex, are you coming back to the apartment?"

"No, I'm going to grandfather's, I mean, my house. I want to sleep in my own bed tonight."

"Our boy did very good, didn't he?"

"Yes, Dad. Kiri is very brave and helpful. He's a good kid. Tomorrow we'll speak to social services and start the adoption process."

My father gave his big-bear grin and hugged me. "Malenkaya, I knew you'd see it my way." It was nearly ten p.m. when we reached the store. My dad picked up Kiri in his arms. "We'll see you tomorrow."

Hunter sat up in the seat, watching Kiri and then looking back at me. Then he lay back down. I watched as my father carried Kiri into the store.

I gave the driver my address and then poured a glass of Stoli. I took a couple of sips and laid my head back, petting Hunter's head. He was lying on my lap now. "You're such a good boy, Hunter. I'm so proud of you. I'm so glad you could see Russia."

I watched out the window as we drove down the Eisenhower, heading to Oak Park. It was dark and a light snow was falling. It was almost December. I thought about what would be Kiri's first Christmas and how my father would enjoy watching him open presents. He'd always wanted a son, and I didn't know if I'd ever give him a grandson. I thought about my grandfather and how much I missed him. How much I wanted to walk into his house and show him the diamond and tell him the story of the salt mines. Tell him the story of the necklace. I thought about Minna and everything Erik had told me about her and about how I'd miss her. All I had left in the world was my father, a young Cambodian boy, my dog and cat. Then I thought about Erik. I felt the ring around my thumb. I twisted it back and forth so I could feel the friction on my skin.

We pulled in front of the house. The whole block was dark, especially the red brick farmhouse. I thanked the driver. Gathering my bag and Hunter, I went up the long driveway that led to the front door.

I fiddled with my keys, not being able to see the lock in the dark. I finally found the hole and opened the door. I threw my backpack onto the console table. I flipped on the light switch. It clicked but there was no light. I flipped it again. Still no light. It was cold in the house. The old electrical box full of fuses must have blown. First thing I'd do when I started renovating would be to replace the fuses with circuit breakers.

For now the fireplace would have to do. I went into the living room and loaded some kindling and logs into the fireplace. I struck a match and watched the fire slowly catch. The orange glow of flames filled the room. Hunter growled behind me. "Hunter, what's—?" Before I could finish my words, I turned to see someone sitting in my grandfather's red leather wing-back chair in the corner by the wall of bookcases.

I reached for my boot knife, but before I could throw it, Minna stood up and walked into the light. "Alexandra," she said, smiling.

I dropped my knife. "Minna?"

"Alexandra, I've been so worried." She walked across the room and hugged me.

I hesitated, not knowing if she were a ghost. And then I hugged her, feeling her slight figure in my arms. I let myself believe she was real. "Minna, we've all been looking for you. Your apartment? The blood?"

"Sit down, Alexandra."

I sat on the couch by the fire. She sat next to me, holding my hand between both her hands, her diamond solitaire refracting the firelight with a brilliant orange-white glow. "My dear, so much has happened. After I found your grandfather, I felt like someone was following me. I would see a man, just a glimpse of a man, mind you. If I was at the grocery store or around the corner from my building, I could never make him out but felt him watching me. I was worried." As Minna spoke, I felt an unease creep over me, a shadow. I touched her diamond. My head began to pound; she continued, "Oh my dear, there's so much in my past that you don't know about, even your grandfather didn't know. Many people would be happy to see me dead. I didn't want you or your father to be in danger, so I called Erik to come get me. He's the only other person I trust." My flashing migraine began. Lights swirling in my eyes, moving pictures but the pictures were not the story that Minna was telling me but an alternate movie. Minna continued talking. "I went home to pack, and that's when the man broke in. I was in my bedroom. He didn't say a word. He came at me with terrifying eyes. I was so scared. You can imagine, right? Not thinking, I reached onto the nightstand and grabbed my crystal vase. I hit him in the head. There was so much blood. I didn't take anything. I ran out of my apartment." Minna started crying. She reached in the sleeve of her long coat and pulled out her linen handkerchief, dotting her eyes.

I put my arm around her. "It's okay." As Minna spoke, I thought of my mother and her migraines and her visions. My father and grandfather wouldn't admit the truth—that my mother had the gift of sight. They wouldn't admit that she'd passed it to me. I could tell Minna was lying.

"I was so worried about myself, about you. I couldn't wait for Erik. I left. I got on a greyhound bus, the first one leaving Chicago that drove for days. I wound up in some small town outside of Scottsdale, Arizona. I was afraid to contact you. I finally called Katrina, and she told me that you'd left Gem with her and went to Ekaterinburg. Then I understood."

I grabbed Minna's hand and touched her diamond. I knew the truth. "Understood what, Minna?"

"The necklace. Ekaterinburg is where the Romanovs were assassinated."

"What are you talking about, Minna?"

"The story your grandfather told about the necklace and the Grand Duke and Catherine Ruskova."

"My grandfather never knew her name. None of us did."

Minna became quiet.

"What are you doing here, Minna?"

"Alexandra, I came to make sure you were safe and to find out what you found in the salt mines."

"How do you know about the salt mines, Minna?"

Minna's face turned from a sweet old woman's face—the face of a mentor—to the face I'd seen in my vision. She turned from a trusted friend I'd known since I was a little girl into an angry bitter woman. "I want to know what you found." This time when she spoke her words were harsh and guttural. Her hand squeezed mine tightly almost to the point of pain.

Hunter, who was lying by the fire, popped up his head and gave a low growl.

"Shut up, dog!" she commanded.

I tried to slowly pull my hand away from her grip, but I couldn't. "You killed him, didn't you?"

"Killed who?"

"You killed Ivan. Otherwise, he would have contacted me. He's dead, isn't he?" Now she squeezed my hand harder. The Viking ring on my thumb tore into my index finger, causing it to bleed.

"What are you talking about, Minna?"

"Ivan was my best agent—in the 1980s before all this new Russian federation, back when we were still Soviets. If he hasn't contacted me by now, that means he's dead."

"You sent him after me?"

Minna reached into her other sleeve, but instead of pulling out another handkerchief, she pulled out a Glock 380. "When your grandfather told me he'd found the necklace—the necklace I've been looking for all my life, I had to see it. I had to know its secret, but he said he was keeping it for you, for your wedding day. He wanted the next story of the necklace to be about you and your husband. He wouldn't even show it to me. He wanted you to be the first one to see it on your wedding day. Stupid old man! I sent Ivan to get answers out of your grandfather. Not to kill him. But Ivan went too far. After he was done, he brought me the necklace. Once I'd deciphered the code on the necklace, it was worthless to me. Out of respect for your grandfather, I gave you the necklace; after all, it was meant for you. Once you started going after the treasure, I couldn't have that. You have to understand. My father searched all his life for the imperial treasure not knowing that the necklace he pulled off his whore wife held the secret."

"Minna, what are you saying?"

"My father, General Yurokov! The traitor to the imperial court but not a traitor—a hero! He helped the Bolsheviks start the revolution and start the Soviet people. He's a hero of the people, and they thanked him by sending him to the United States as an ambassador. This great war hero, this brilliant military man ends up pushing papers in Washington DC. His only saving grace—boxes and boxes of correspondence with the KGB, hunting down any lead, no matter how small, about the hundreds of millions of dollars of lost imperial jewels. He died an angry, sad man. And that's where I took over. I joined the KGB and searched every database I could find for the jeweler named Volkov who'd made the necklace and anything that would lead to the Grand Duke and the treasure. Yes, your family. It took me years of tracking down every lead until I found records from Ellis Island in 1917. A Russian man named Volkov, entering the United States, changing his name to Kustodia, and then I found Kustodia jewelry and your grandfather."

"You're insane."

"Give it to me! Give me what you found. Where's the treasure?" Her eyes were wild and lost. All I could see through the darkness was the reflection from the fire in them.

Hunter rose up, growling, baring his teeth. Minna pointed the gun at Hunter's heart.

"No!" I screamed, pushing her arm. The gun fired, missing Hunter, the bullet grazing the bricks of the fireplace. I pulled Minna to the floor. I could feel a sharp burning pain slowly sliding into my lower back, deeper, deeper. I rolled over on the floor and pulled the knife out of my back, coughing, dizzy. Minna rose to her feet, quicker than I could imagine for a woman of her age. Hunter leaped at her. She punched Hunter in the chest, knocking him over, sending him rolling onto the floor, whimpering.

Minna turned to me and aimed the gun at my head. I lay back on my heels. I felt darkness filling my eyes. I was passing out. I caught myself on the floor as I was falling and felt my bloody boot knife that Minna had stuck in my back. With my eyes barely open, I flung the knife. It found its target, piercing Minna's heart. She dropped the gun and fell to the floor, dead. I crawled over to Hunter. "Hunter, my brave boy. Hunter." He lay on his side, whimpering but licking my face. "Are you okay, boy?" His tail wagged, hitting the floor hard.

The last thing I remember was trying to reach for the phone on the end table, and then the darkness closed in.

Chapter Twenty-three

Darkness. My pupils fully dilate searching for any last remnant of light; there is none. I hear voices but there's only darkness. I can't feel my body. I have no sense of direction. I don't know if I'm alive or dead. Time passes without me.

A burst of white light and then I see my father's face. I'm alive. All I hear is the beep of the monitors. Kiri jumps on the bed and hugs me. "Easy, boy, easy," my father says.

"It's okay, Dad. Really, it's okay."

My father kneels down, kissing my head.

"Hunter?" I ask.

"Hunter's fine. You must rest now. There'll be time to talk later." My father kisses my forehead.

"Miss Alex," Kiri whispers, taking my hand in his. I feel the cold weight of the hundred-carat diamond as he places it in my palm.

"Come on, boy," my father says, placing his arm around Kiri's shoulder. "Alex needs her rest." My father switches the light off in the room, closing the door behind them.

I close my grip around the diamond. My fingertips tingle and then the burst of electricity shoots through me. My head pounds. I close my eyes and then the movie begins.

THE END

ABOUT THE AUTHOR

 After years as a reporter, Vicki Vass turned in her reporter's notebook to write about her passion for gems. Vicki Vass has written more than 1,400 articles for the *Chicago Tribune* as well as *Woman's World*, the *Daily Herald* and *Home & Away*.

Her other series, Antique Hunters Mystery series, is based on her other passion for antique shopping, and features the adventures of real-life antique hunters Anne and CC. Her Neighborhood Watch series chronicles the not-quite-true events of her Chicago suburban neighborhood.

She lives outside Chicago with her writer/musician husband, Brian, twenty-year-old photojournalist son Tony, cats, Pixel and Terra, Australian shepherd Bandit, and seven koi.

Learn more at vickivass.com or follow her on Facebook at facebook.com/vickivassauthor.

ALSO BY VICKI VASS

Antique Hunters Mysteries
Murder for Sale
Pickin' Murder
Killer Finds
Key to a Murder

Neighborhood Watch Mysteries
The Postman Is Late

Witch Cat Mystery
Bloodline

Eleven: 1

visit: vickivass.com
To win new releases, and other cozy stuff!

www.ingramcontent.com/pod-product-compliance
Lightning Source LLC
Chambersburg PA
CBHW020635180626
46816CB00003B/972

* 9 7 8 0 9 9 8 9 8 9 3 1 0 *